E.C. Priber

The Vineyards in Napa County

Being the report of E.C. Priber, commissioner for the Napa District

E.C. Priber

The Vineyards in Napa County
Being the report of E.C. Priber, commissioner for the Napa District

ISBN/EAN: 9783337423018

Printed in Europe, USA, Canada, Australia, Japan

Cover: Foto ©Andreas Hilbeck / pixelio.de

More available books at **www.hansebooks.com**

THE

VINEYARDS IN NAPA COUNTY;

BEING

THE REPORT OF E. C. PRIBER, COMMISSIONER FOR THE NAPA DISTRICT,

TO THE

BOARD OF STATE VITICULTURAL COMMISSIONERS OF CALIFORNIA.

———

PUBLISHED BY THE BOARD OF STATE VITICULTURAL
COMMISSIONERS.

SACRAMENTO:

STATE OFFICE, : : : : : A. J. JOHNSTON, SUPT. STATE PRINTING.

1893.

OFFICERS AND MEMBERS OF THE BOARD.

INTRODUCTION.

The present report on the condition of the vineyards of Napa County was undertaken by the Board of State Viticultural Commissioners with a view of ascertaining what decrease in the acreage planted in vines in that county has been caused by the phylloxera in the past two years, as well as to give as much information as possible regarding the success of the various resistant stocks in different soils, etc., and other matters pertaining to viticulture in the county of interest to grape growers, wine makers, and wine merchants.

In 1890, when the last census was made, Napa County reported 18,229 acres planted in vines. The present report shows 16,651½ acres. It will thus be seen that the decrease has been very considerable.

The phylloxera is reported to have reached a point about three miles above St. Helena, and it can be but a question of a short time until the Calistoga vineyards suffer as have those of the lower valley.

At present there are 507 vineyards reported in Napa County, and of these 244, or nearly half, report the existence of phylloxera. This will give an idea of what can be expected to occur to the vineyards of the entire valley within a few years. Wherever resistants have not been planted, the death of the vines appears only a question of a short time.

In the tables which follow, the acreage reported as infested by phylloxera is certainly misleading, as is also the reported acreage good for one more crop, the acreage that will be dug up for causes other than phylloxera, and probably the cooperage. It is difficult to secure correct information on such points; vineyardists are loth to give such information, as well as to give information as to stocks of wine on hand.

The reports of wine stocks were given in confidence. The different cellars reported an aggregate of slightly over 5,000,000 gallons of wine in the valley. The stocks of two cellars in Napa had to be estimated, as well as the cooperage in the same, the owners refusing to supply such information.

It is naturally to be expected that in making such a canvass errors will occur. If any are noted, the vineyardists affected will please notify me. There is no disposition to do any one injustice, nor to misrepresent any one. Any corrections sent in will be printed, and distributed, for insertion in this book.

The canvass was made by Mr. A. Warren Robinson, of Napa, under direction of Commissioner E. C. Priber and the Executive Committee of the Board. In this work the following blank was used:

.... COUNTY.

.... DISTRICT IN COUNTY.

Name and address, ...

Total acres in vines, ...

Acres in bearing, ...

Acres in wine grapes, ...

Acres in table grapes, ...

Acres in raisin grapes, ...

Will be replanted, and how many acres, ...

Acres at present infested by Phylloxera. { Good for only one crop more, ... acres.
Total, ... acres. { Good for more than one crop more, ... acres.

Acres planted to Resistants. { Riparia, ... acres. { On Riparia, ... acres. { Which varieties succeed best? ....
Total, ... acres. { Rupestris, ... acres. { Which varieties have not succeeded? ....
{ Lenoir, ... acres. { On Rupestris, ... acres. { Which varieties succeed best? ....
{ Other varieties, ... acres. { Which varieties have not succeeded? ....
{ On Lenoir, ... acres. { Which varieties succeed best? ....
{ Which varieties have not succeeded? ....
Acres planted to Resistants (same { Grafted and in bearing, ... acres. { On other varieties (name { Which varieties succeed best? ....
as preceding). { Grafted and not bearing, ... acres. { them), ... acres. { Which varieties have not succeeded? ....
Total, ... acres. { Not yet grafted, ... acres.

Character of the soil of the vineyard: ....

How is the vineyard situated—low lying, upland, or mountain? ....

What is exposure to sun and wind? ....

Which of the European varieties have proved most resistant? ....

How have the vineyards that have been attacked been handled? ....

Crop in 1892? ....

Stock of wine on hand, in gallons? ....

Total quantity of cooperage, ... gallons: { Oak cooperage, ... gallons.
{ Redwood cooperage, ... gallons.

Remarks: ....

In tabulating the returns thus obtained, the county was divided into five districts: First, in and around Napa; second, farther up, from Yountville to Rutherford; third, in and about St. Helena; fourth, Chiles and Conn Valleys; and fifth, in and about Calistoga.

The recapitulation of the total is as follows:

NAPA COUNTY.

Total number of vineyards	507.
Vineyards reporting phylloxera	244.
Total acres in vines	16,651½ acres.
Acres in bearing	14,240½ acres.
Will replant this season	406½ acres.
Will be dug up for causes other than phylloxera	184 acres.
Infested by phylloxera	2,246 acres.
Same good for but one crop more	756 acres.

Planted to Resistants, 2,007¼ acres, as follows:	Riparia	1,698½ acres.
	Lenoir	245¾ acres.
	Rupestris	19 acres.
	Californica	35 acres.
	Æstivalis	9 acres.

Planted to Resistants (same as above), 2,007¼ acres	Grafted and in bearing	842½ acres.
	Grafted and not bearing	591 acres.
	Not yet grafted	573¾ acres.

Crop, 1892	27,083 tons.

Cooperage, 12,989,000 gallons	Oak	3,662,500 gallons.
	Redwood	9,326,500 gallons.

The recapitulation of the different districts in the county is as follows:

NAPA DISTRICT.

Total number of vineyards, 91.
Vineyards reporting phylloxera, 53.
Total acres in vines, 3,636.
Acres in bearing, 2,715.
Will replant this season, 103 acres.
Will be dug up other than for phylloxera, 75 acres.
Infested by phylloxera, 455 acres; of which 154 will bear but one crop more.
Planted to resistants, 1,157 acres; of which 1,000 acres are in Riparia, 138 Lenoir, and 19 Rupestris.
Planted to resistants (same as above), 1,157 acres; of which 515½ are grafted and bearing, 451½ are grafted and not bearing, and 190 not yet grafted.
Crop 1892, 5,579 tons.
Cooperage, 3,101,000 gallons; of which 506,000 is oak and 2,595,000 redwood.

YOUNTVILLE DISTRICT.

Total number of vineyards, 81.
Vineyards reporting phylloxera, 64.
Total acres in vines, 2,706.
Acres in bearing, 2,054.
Will replant this season, 142 acres.
Will be dug up for reasons other than phylloxera, 75 acres.
Infested by phylloxera, 701 acres; of which 261 will bear but one crop more.
Planted to resistants, 497 acres; of which 431 acres are in Riparia, 31 acres in Lenoir, and 35 acres in Californica.
Planted to resistants (same as above), 497 acres; of which 206 are grafted and bearing, 64 grafted but not bearing, and 227 not yet grafted.
Crop 1892, 4,605 tons.
Cooperage, 2,489,000 gallons; of which 411,000 is oak and 2,078,000 redwood.

ST. HELENA DISTRICT.

Total number of vineyards, 219.
Vineyards reporting phylloxera, 119.
Total acres in vines, 7,445½.
Acres in bearing, 6,784.
Will replant this season, 108½ acres.
Will be dug up for causes other than phylloxera, 34 acres.
Infested by phylloxera, 1,042 acres; of which 335 will bear but one crop more.
Planted to resistants, 209¾ acres; of which 145 acres are in Riparia and 64¾ in Lenoir.

Planted to resistants (same as above), 259¾ acres; of which 35 are grafted and in bearing, 58½ grafted but not bearing, and 116¼ not yet grafted.
Crop of 1892, 12,604 tons.
Cooperage, 6,145,000 gallons; of which 2,275,000 is oak and 3,870,000 redwood.

CHILES AND CONN VALLEYS.

Total number of vineyards, 28.
Vineyards reporting phylloxera, 7.
Total acres in vines, 814.
Acres in bearing, 767½.
Will replant this season, 13 acres.
Infested by phylloxera, 46 acres; of which 16 will bear but one crop more.
Planted to resistants, 38½ acres; of which 27½ are in Riparia, 9 in Estivalis, and 2 in Lenoir.
Planted to resistants (same as above), 38½ acres; of which 11 are grafted and in bearing, 17 grafted but not bearing, and 10½ acres not yet grafted.
Crop of 1892, 1,091 tons.
Cooperage, 379,000 gallons; of which 157,500 gallons is oak and 221,500 gallons is redwood.

CALISTOGA DISTRICT.

Total number of vineyards, 88.
Vineyard reporting phylloxera, 1.
Total acres in vines, 2,044.
Acres in bearing, 1,920.
Will replant this season, 40 acres.
Infested by phylloxera, 2 acres.
Planted to resistants, 105 acres; of which 95 are in Riparia and 10 in Lenoir.
Planted to resistants (same as above), 105 acres; of which 75 are grafted and in bearing, and 30 not yet grafted.
Crop of 1892, 3,204 tons.
Cooperage, 875,000 gallons; of which 313,000 is oak and 562,000 is redwood.

WINFIELD SCOTT,
Secretary Board of State Viticultural Commissioners.

NAPA, December 1, 1892.

To the Board of State Viticultural Commissioners:

GENTLEMEN: I herewith submit the report of A. Warren Robinson, containing remarks on the census of Napa County, and the census obtained by him.

Respectfully,

E. C. PRIBER,
Commissioner for the Napa District.

NAPA, December 1, 1892.

To E. C. PRIBER, *Viticultural Commissioner for the Napa District:*

DEAR SIR: I beg leave to submit the following viticultural report for Napa County, as per your instructions and formulas furnished.

Every vineyard portion of Napa County has been visited and inspected, and all the information possible gained bearing on viticultural matters, especially anything of interest regarding resistant vines.

Since my last report, two years ago, vineyards in this county have been greatly lessened in number and in area, in many portions of the county. Commencing ten years ago in the lower end of Napa Valley, and supposed to have been brought from Sonoma Valley, the phylloxera has spread almost the entire length of the valley in the direction of the prevailing wind. Two years ago a few vineyards in the Napa District and some in the Yountville District were infested. Since that time it has spread with great rapidity. In many cases vineyards of considerable extent have, in the meantime, almost or wholly disappeared. This will account for the smaller number of vineyards reported this year.

No remedy to prevent the spread of the disease has been discovered. In no vineyards visited, with the exception of one or two, has there been any special treatment, and this explains why answers to the question bearing on this matter do not appear. The exceptions mentioned were where a few vines were treated with sulphate of iron, in the proportion of one pound of the sulphate to ten gallons of water. This was applied, when the ground was wet, to the stocks, with a swab, with beneficial results. How long this benefit will last is a question time alone will solve.

In almost every vineyard visited, where the phylloxera has made any headway, the vines were allowed to stand without treatment, the disease taking its course. When the vines were dead, or nearly so, they were pulled up. Rarely have resistants or other vines been set out in their place. In the last two years very few new vineyards have been planted—none, in fact—nor will new vineyards be planted or old ones be reset, except in a comparatively few instances, this coming winter and spring. As a whole, vineyardists have come to the conclusion that any special treatment is useless and a waste of time. About ten years ago experiments in the matter of curing phylloxera-diseased vines were made in the vineyards of H. Hagen and Mr. Bauer, but they proved of little or no avail.

Frequently vineyards have gone very suddenly, the phylloxera having, evidently, obtained a strong hold upon the roots and showing very little effect upon the vines until nearly the end.

Judging from the experience of the past few years, it may be safe to say that within the space of three or four years a very large proportion of the vineyards south of the Calistoga District will have been destroyed. A very large proportion of these will not be replanted, for past experience has proved that it would be folly to set out European vines on their own roots, and very few vineyardists can afford to wait the four or five years required to establish resistant vines, no income being derived from the vineyard in the meantime. I found this to be the prevailing sentiment in all phylloxera-infested localities.

Besides this there is no encouragement to replant on account of the poor outlook for the wine industry. Prices have ruled low for some years, and are now two or three cents below the figure desired. The cellars are, in many instances, overstocked with wine of the vintages of the present and previous years. Some men are carrying four vintages; a great many one or two.

The phylloxera, almost invariably, has attacked vineyards in spots. Appearing in the center of a block it spreads in circles of varying diameters, and then will jump a rod or more and appear in the center of another block. Rarely, if ever, does it sweep a direct swath through a vineyard. Some vineyardists are confident that the insect, coming to the surface at certain seasons of the year, flies a short distance. Others think the insect is carried along by the plow. Invariably the disease spreads in the direction of the prevailing winds, which, throughout Napa Valley, are from south to north, or, more correctly, from the southwest up the valley. Exposure to the sun has been given in noting hill vineyards, but on level lands it has been omitted, as exposure to the sun there is always direct, and the wind usually as stated.

South of Lodi Station vineyards generally are badly infested with phylloxera, excepting on Spring Mountain. North of Lodi Station, they are almost invariably intact. In no vineyard in the vicinity of Calistoga, so far as could be seen from extended observation, could I see traces of phylloxera, yet vineyardists in this locality, while rejoicing that their vines are not diseased, will not be surprised if the destructive insect should appear any season. The same may be said of vineyards on Spring Mountain, to the northwest of St. Helena.

The vintage in this county was from one half to two thirds shorter than usual this year, owing, in a considerable measure, to the ravages of the phylloxera, much to killing frosts in the spring, and quite a little to very hot weather in June. All this, coupled with low prices, has discouraged many vineyardists.

Acting in accordance with your instructions: to pay much attention to the results of the planting of resistant vines, and the success attending their cultivation, I made extensive inquiries in all sections of the county. Comparatively few vineyardists have set out resistants of any kind. It is only here and there that owners of vineyards have made the experiment, if experiment it may longer be called. Vineyardmen of small or even moderate means think they cannot afford to wait the time required for the vines to grow, to be grafted, and to bear fruit.

But several men of keen observation, after careful investigation, are persuaded that resistants are a success. Riparia and Lenoir are the principal varieties propagated. Of Rupestris there is none to speak of, and of Californica very little. Riparia holds the foremost place in the estimation of nine tenths of those who have used resistants at all. This variety has been found to grow well and successfully resist the phylloxera on high lands as well as on lower levels. In some vineyards, European vines, grafted on Riparia roots, have borne good crops, and the owners are well pleased with the outlook. Lenoir has been used on low grounds, and in many, probably in all cases, has proved a failure. "Lenoir does not bear wet feet," as Mr. E. P. Palmer says.

This gentleman, after extended and careful observation, study, and experiment, lasting through a period of several years, and whose judgment in the premises is thereby entitled to great consideration, pronounces, emphatically, in favor of the Riparia. "I consider the man who plants Lenoir is taking chances," said he. A committee of vineyardists, of which Mr. Palmer was a member, were last spring appointed by the St. Helena Viticultural Association to visit and critically inspect vineyards, both in Napa and Sonoma Counties, in which resistants, for any considerable time, had been planted, and said in their report: "We condemn the planting of Lenoir on lowest soils. While Riparia would not be in its native element in such soils, yet having shown a better adaptation for cold, wet, and heavy land, it stands preëminently in the lead as a resistant."

Mr. Charles Krug, with his eleven or twelve years' experience with resistants, advised setting out Riparia.

I found, with but one or two exceptions, that where replanting is to be done this winter or next spring, Riparias will be used as resistant stocks. Once in awhile a man was found who favored Lenoir because of its more rapid growth. It can be grafted much earlier than the slower growing Riparia.

To sum up observations upon this point, it may be said that while in some soils Lenoir may prove a resistant, Riparia, on the whole, is esteemed the best resistant stock to plant. Experiments carefully conducted, and critical observation, have proved conclusively that the Riparia is preëminently the best resistant planted in this county. Of this there seems to be no doubt.

Will resistants be generally planted as vineyards are destroyed by phylloxera? This question has, in a measure, been answered on foregoing pages. In the very great majority of cases, no; in the few, yes. Even many who consider resistants a success, will be deterred by reason of expense and the long "waiting time." The result will inevitably be, as previously stated, that only a few years will elapse before bearing vineyards in this county will be of limited number. The resulting loss to this county will be very great, and would be difficult to estimate, as the hard labor and the expense of establishing vineyards and building capacious wine cellars, especially north of Yountville, has been very great.

The foregoing remarks apply to hill vineyards as well as to those in the different valleys in the county. Napa Valley, with its surrounding hills, has not alone suffered in this matter, though vineyards in other valleys in the county are few in number and of limited extent. In Gordon Valley, within the last two years, vineyards have been devastated by phylloxera. In Berryessa Valley little attention has been paid to the cultivation of the vine. The small vineyards of Pope Valley are growing smaller. In Wooden and Capelle Valleys there are no vineyards worthy of note. These smaller valleys are so difficult of access and the mountain roads leading to them are so long and rough, that land owners have been deterred from planting vineyards. Perhaps it is as well. Foss Valley vineyards, all of limited area, are still in fair condition. On the Suscol hills, since my last report, whole vineyards have been uprooted, because of the rapid devastation by the ubiquitous phylloxera.

Very many vineyardists fully appreciate the efforts of the Commission to spread information regarding the success that has attended the planting of resistants. They will gladly avail themselves of published facts and the experience of those who have planted resistants to any extent. It is evident this useful information will be of great practical benefit to all concerned. The last reports of the California Viticultural Commission, issued this fall, have been extensively circulated in this county, and, by a large majority of vineyardists, were gladly received.

I have endeavored to carefully and conscientiously follow the instructions given me. I have made a complete canvass of the vine-growing districts of the county. The results of my observations and inquiries are embodied in this report and contained in the blanks furnished. While I would not act the pessimist, but would give as hopeful a report as possible, it is useless to hide the fact that our vineyards are melting away, as the mist before the morning sun.

In resistant stocks the only remedy for preserving our vineyards has been found. It has already been stated that vineyards so rooted will be comparatively few. I think an investigation of the matters submitted, made two or three years hence, will prove the facts stated and forecasts made to have been true.

I trust my efforts to follow and carry out your instructions will meet with your approval and will give complete satisfaction.

Respectfully submitted.

A. W. ROBINSON.

The above report is indorsed and submitted to the Commissioners.

E. C. PRIBER,
Commissioner for the Napa District.

SUPPLEMENTAL REPORT.

NAPA, December 10, 1892.

It would be exceedingly difficult for any one to accurately judge of the amount of vineyard acreage in this county now infested by phylloxera, even approximately. Some vineyards, and they are not a few, are entirely destroyed, and the remnants of quite a number will be dug up this winter. But it has been noticed in the past that many vine-yards have suddenly shown signs of the presence of the destroying insect, and whole blocks of vines have died in a very short time, indi-cating, evidently, that the phylloxera had, unknown and often unsur-mised, been for some time hard at work at the roots.

So it is to-day. Vines that show no signs of disease may soon be swept away. It is for this reason that hardly any one can judge accu-rately of the acreage of vines now infected. Those that are badly diseased, or even to a fair degree, can be detected by the practiced eye, if signs of this condition of things appear above ground. But detection often comes first when the vines are thoroughly diseased.

Therefore, it may be safely stated that the results of the ravages of the phylloxera in our vineyards during the year or two to come cannot now be accurately estimated, and the figures given in this report do not begin to show the vastness of the injury now working and to follow within even two years.

Since the time resistants were first planted in this county, different parties have had much expensive experience in grafting foreign varieties upon them. Failure attended many of the first trials, but, profiting by past efforts, grafting is performed, if proper care be taken in every detail of its operation, successfully. "In my vineyard 99 per cent of grafts have taken and grown vigorously," said one vineyardist.

Many of the failures in years gone by were due to too deep and careless grafting. The soil was dug away from the resistant vine sev-eral inches, and the stock cut off some distance from the surface. Where this method was practiced a very large per cent of the grafts often died. The union of stock and scion was imperfect. In cases where the scion was not inserted so low down, but still a few inches below the surface, failure resulted because the roots the scion threw off were not removed, through inattention or lack of knowledge. The consequence was that as they grew they forced the scion out of the stock, and failure resulted.

The best success now attained by some persons who have had much experience in grafting, is to insert the scion in the resistant stock quite near or at the surface of the ground. Care should always be taken to see that any rootlets the scion may throw off are removed. If per-mitted to grow, the phylloxera may, as often has been the case, prey upon these roots and destroy the vine. When this occurs, the resistant stock has frequently been condemned, though unjustly, as non-resistant.

When due care has been taken, success has universally attended grafting upon resistant stocks. Inner bark of stock and scion must be sure to meet, and after tying, the earth should be firmly pressed around the graft. If the cleft graft is used and but one scion is inserted, the cleft to one side of the scion will readily heal, although there has been some dispute on this point.

The method of inserting the scion in the side of the stock, at an angle, allowing the resistant vine above the graft to continue its growth until the union is perfect, then to remove that portion of the vine above the scion, has been tried, but not always with success. The theory may be good, but the result often has been that the wind would sway the vine back and forth, and the graft would be forced out.

Again, it has been found best to allow the resistant stock to attain good size before grafting, as, if the graft is inserted too early, there will not be sufficient strength in the stock to support the scion; or the scion may overgrow the stock and the result be far from what is desired. But where due care is taken in all the essentials, grafts grow readily, rapidly, and yield bountifully, even bearing the first year or two. Said a vineyardist who has had abundant success in grafting resistants: "I took this fall, from a scion inserted in Riparia stock last spring, eight pounds of excellent grapes." Another, who has had considerable experience in grafting, said: "From two-year old Sauvignon Vert grafts inserted in Riparia stocks, I gathered this fall as high as thirty-five pounds of grapes to a graft."

In more than one instance inquiry elicited the information that it was preferable to plant resistant cuttings where they were to permanently remain in the vineyard. If planted in the nursery and transplanted when the roots had well grown, there is, of necessity, more or less of a check to the growth of the vine. The experience of one practical vineyardist of many years' observation has been that cuttings have, in a year or two, overtaken rooted vines that were transplanted. On the other hand, there are those who contend that it is easier to care for the resistant cuttings in the nursery until they are well rooted, and at much less expense, than to plant cuttings at once in the vineyard. There are those who favor the one plan—some the other. But many strong and unanswerable arguments are presented in favor of the method first mentioned.

What is required in successful grafting is patience, care, and watchfulness, at the time of grafting and for some months thereafter. If this system is pursued, success should attend grafting, as has been proved conclusively by the experience of many vineyardists in this county.

A. WARREN ROBINSON.

REPORT ON VINEYARDS.

John Aroth, Napa.—Total acres, 15, of which 9 are in bearing; will replant 2 acres; acres infested with phylloxera, 2, all to be dug out; planted to Riparia, 6 acres, of which 3 are in bearing and 3 grafted but not bearing; Zinfandel grafts have succeeded, but Muscats have not; soil sandy loam; vineyard upland; exposure southeast; crop, 14 tons.

Bank of Napa, Napa.—Total, 105 acres; in bearing, 90 acres; will replant 5 or 10 acres; infested by phylloxera, scattering, about 20 acres, of which 10 are good for only one crop; planted to Riparia, 33 acres, of which 9 acres are grafted and in bearing, 4 acres grafted and not bearing, and 20 acres not yet grafted; Sauvignon Vert, Semillon, and all other varieties grafted, have succeeded well; soil gravelly loam; vineyard upland; exposure west. The Burgundy and Chasselas Fontainebleau have proved most resistant; no special pains taken with vines attacked. Crop, 220 tons; cooperage, 150,000 gallons, all redwood.

L. Bauchero, Napa.—Total, 40 acres; in bearing, 35; infested by phylloxera, 5; good for only one crop more, 3; planted to Lenoir, 5, which are grafted but not bearing; soil rocky loam; vineyard mountain; exposure southwest; Zinfandel has resisted fairly well; crop, 75 tons; cooperage, 40,000 gallons, of which 5,000 is oak and 35,000 redwood.

Bauer Estate, Napa.—Total, 60 acres; in bearing, 50 acres; will replant 8 acres; planted to Riparia, 30 acres, and to Lenoir 30 acres, all of which are not yet grafted; soil loam; vineyard mountain; exposure southwest; Tokay has proved most resistant; crop, 80 tons.
This vineyard is situated in Napa redwoods. The resistants are planted between rows of the vinifera. If phylloxera appears, old vines will be dug up, leaving resistants in good condition.

J. A. Baxter, Napa.—Total, 115 acres; in bearing, 100 acres in table grapes, 5 acres; planted to Riparia, 15 acres, which are not yet grafted; soil heavy loam; vineyard upland; exposure west and north; crop, 124 tons; stock of wine on hand, 24,000 gallons; cooperage, 40,000 gallons, of which 10,000 is oak and 30,000 redwood.
Riparia stands highest in estimation as resistant.

J. J. Bergen, Napa.—Total, 10 acres; in bearing, 8 acres; infested by phylloxera, 4 acres, half of which is good for only one crop; no resistants; soil light loam; vineyard upland; exposure southwest; crop, 15 tons.
This vineyard will be dug up in a year or two.

B. Boetto, Napa.—Total, 10 acres; all in bearing; infested by phylloxera, 3 acres, of which 1 will bear only one crop more; soil loam; vineyard upland; crop, 20 tons; cooperage, 20,000 gallons, all redwood.

F. Borreo, Napa.—Total, 50 acres, of which 40 are in bearing; will replant 2 acres; planted to Lenoir, 4 acres, all of which are grafted but not bearing; the grafts succeed equally well; soil rocky black loam; exposure south; Zinfandel, Grey Riesling, and Burgundy, of European varieties, are most resistant in the order named; crop, 100 tons; cooperage, 80,000 gallons, of which 10,000 is oak and 70,000 redwood.
This vineyard is situated near the Napa Soda Springs, a few hundred feet above the valley. Here Riparia has almost utterly failed, whereas Lenoir does exceedingly well.

John Brandlein, Napa.—Total, 12 acres; all in bearing; will replant 4 or 5 acres; soil loam; vineyard upland; exposure southeast; crop, 16 tons.

M. Buchli, Napa.—Total, 15 acres, all in bearing; soil loam; vineyard upland; exposure east and south; crop, 25 tons.

A. Carboni, Napa.—Total, 40 acres; in bearing, 30 acres; infested by phylloxera, 25 acres, of which 10 acres are good for only one crop more; soil loam; vineyard low lying; exposure southwest; no special treatment for phylloxera; crop, 100 tons; cooperage, 10,000 gallons, all redwood.
Mr. Carboni is much discouraged with the outlook. Two years ago the vineyard was in fine condition; now it is rapidly dying out.

C. Carpy & Co., Napa.—Cooperage (estimated), 1,250,000 gallons, of which 200,000 is oak and 1,050,000 redwood.

Mrs. E. Castle, Napa.—Total, 7 acres; soil loam; vineyard mountain; exposure south; crop, 25 tons.

H. B. Chase, Napa.—Total, 80 acres; in bearing, 70 acres; will replant 10 acres; crop, 271 tons.

2—N

George Chatterly, Napa.—Total, 18 acres; in bearing, 15 acres; infested by phylloxera, 4 acres, of which half is good for only one crop more; planted to Riparia, 1 acre, which is grafted to Zinfandel, and is in bearing; variety has succeeded well; soil loam; vineyard low lying; no great care given attacked vines; crop, 15 tons.

H. Connell, Napa.—Total, 9 acres; in bearing, 5 acres; infested by phylloxera, 3 acres, of which 2 acres are good for only one crop more; soil loam and gravel; vineyard upland; vineyard treated all alike; crop, 5 tons.

J. H. Cummings, Napa.—Total, 25 acres; all in bearing; soil loam; vineyard upland; exposure south and east; crop, 40 tons.

B. Darms, Napa.—Total, 70 acres; in bearing, 50 acres; will replant 2 acres; infested by phylloxera, 10 acres, half of which is good for only one crop more; planted to Riparia, 10 acres, of which 5 acres are grafted and in bearing, 3 acres grafted but not bearing, and 2 acres not yet grafted; Zinfandel, Mondeuse, and Chasselas have succeeded well on Riparia; soil loam; vineyard upland; exposure east; no special care given diseased vines; crop, 135 tons.
Riparia is in favor at this vineyard. The Lenoir has not succeeded.

James Davis, Napa.—Total, 65 acres; in bearing, 60 acres; vineyard low lying; exposure southeast; all vines in this vineyard attacked by phylloxera have been dug up as soon as the disease was seen; crop, 120 tons.

Charles Dell, Napa.—Total. 20 acres; all in bearing; infested by phylloxera, 2 acres; planted to resistants, 18 acres, of which 13 are in Riparia, 3 in Rupestris, and 2 in Lenoir; all in resistants are grafted and in bearing; the Zinfandel and Mataro do well on the three stocks, and the Muscat has done the poorest; soil rich loam; vineyard upland; exposure northeast; Tokay and Zinfandel have proved most resistant of European varieties; attacked vines were dug out as soon as badly decayed; crop, 50 tons; cooperage, 20,000 gallons, of which 2,000 is oak and 18,000 redwood.

A. S. Domergue, Napa.—Total, 12 acres; all in bearing; soil loam; vineyard upland; crop, 22 tons; cooperage, 15,000 gallons, all redwood.

James Duhig, Napa.—Total, 40 acres; all in bearing; will replant 10 acres; infested by phylloxera, 10 acres, of which 3 acres are good for only one crop more; planted to Riparia, 5 acres, all of which are not yet grafted; soil loam; vineyard upland; exposure east and south; Tokay has proved most resistant; crop, 70 tons.
The resistants are doing very well. This vineyard is on Hinchlea Creek. Several fine vineyards have been killed here by phylloxera within ten or twelve years. It was very near here that phylloxera made its first appearance in Napa County, entering from Sonoma County.

T. H. Epley, Napa.—Total, 8 acres; in bearing, 5½ acres; in table grapes, 8 acres; planted to Riparia, 2½ acres, which are grafted and bearing; Muscat and Thompson's Seedling grafts both succeed very well; soil gravelly; vineyard upland; exposure west and north; crop, 7 tons.
This is about the only vineyard of table grapes in the county. Riparia gives complete satisfaction, but Lenoir is considered very poor.

M. M. Estee, Napa.—Total, 500 acres; in bearing, 350 acres; infested with phylloxera, 50 acres, which will last more than one year; planted to resistants, 150 acres, of which 125 are in Riparia and 25 are Lenoir; grafted and bearing, 50 acres; grafted but not bearing, 75 acres; not grafted, 25 acres; all grafts have succeeded well; soil loam; vineyard rolling; exposure west and southeast; as the disease spread resistants were substituted; cooperage, 200,000 gallons, of which 20,000 is oak and 180,000 redwood.
The resistant vines in this vineyard are doing very well. The Riparia is preferred, and does best on light soil. As the diseased vines are dug up the Riparia will be substituted.

J. H. Fisher, Napa.—Total, 10 acres; in bearing, 10 acres; soil loam; vineyard mountain; exposure southeast; crop, 30 tons; cooperage, 20,000 gallons, of which 15,000 is oak and 5,000 redwood.

P. Flannagan, Napa.—Total, 45 acres; in bearing, 30 acres; will replant 10 acres; very little is infested by phylloxera; planted to Riparia, 15 acres, which are not yet grafted; soil loam; vineyard low lying; Malvoisie has proved most resistant of European varieties; crop, 31 tons.

France & Corterelli, Napa.—Total, 20 acres; all in bearing; infested by phylloxera, 10 acres, of which 3 are good for only one crop more; soil loam; vineyard upland; crop, 37 tons.

F. Frash, Napa.—Total, 24 acres; in bearing, 18 acres; planted to Riparia, 2½ acres, of which 1 acre is grafted and bearing, and 1½ acres grafted but not bearing; Mondeuse has succeeded well on grafts; soil loam; vineyard upland; crop, 25 tons.

P. Fournier, Napa.—Total, 22 acres; all in bearing; infested by phylloxera, 5 acres; soil gravelly; vineyard low lying; crop, 45 tons; cooperage, 60,000 gallons, of which 10,000 is oak and 50,000 redwood.

S. E. Garner, Napa.—Total, 6 acres; all in bearing; soil gravelly loam; vineyard low lying; crop, 10 tons.

C. E. Geddes, Napa.—Total, 5 acres; all in bearing; infested by phylloxera, 2 acres; soil gravelly; vineyard upland; crop, 11 tons.

Mrs. Julia Gift, Napa.—Total, 14 acres; in bearing, 8 acres; infested by phylloxera, 9 acres, of which 4 acres are good for but one crop more; soil light loam; all attacked vines succumb equally and the vines are pulled up as they decay; crop, 8 tons.
This vineyard is fast decaying.

G. W. Gildersleeve, Napa.—Total, 17 acres; infested by phylloxera, 10 acres, of which half is good for only one crop more; vineyard mountain; exposure southwest; all European varieties succumb alike; crop, 18 tons.

G. Gilmetti, Napa.—Total, 5 acres; in bearing, 4 acres; infested by phylloxera, 5 acres, of which 4 acres are good for only one crop more; soil loam; vineyard mountain; exposure west; Zinfandel has proved most resistant of European varieties; crop, 10 tons.

G. Gnepper, Napa.—Total, 18 acres; all in bearing; infested by phylloxera, 4 acres, of which 1 acre is good for only one crop more; soil loam; vineyard upland; crop, 40 tons.

G. E. Goodman, Napa.—Total, 190 acres; in bearing, 180 acres; will replant 8 acres; infested by phylloxera, 15 acres, of which 7 acres are good for only one crop more; planted to resistants, 30 acres, 20 acres of which are grafted and in bearing, 5 acres grafted but not bearing, and 5 acres not yet grafted; varieties of resistant stock: Riparia 25 acres, Rupestris 3 acres, Lenoir 2 acres; the Semillon, Verdot, Burger, Sauvignon Vert, and Cabernet Sauvignon have all done well on Riparia, while both Lenoir and Rupestris have not been successful as stock, the Lenoir especially being too soft; a few Californicas have been tested, but have not succeeded; soil gravelly loam; vineyard low lying; all European varieties succumb alike; the vines are rooted out as soon as infected; crop, 300 tons; cooperage, 200,000 gallons, all redwood.
The land is very rich and all the resistants and grafts look well. The Riparia grows slower than the Lenoir, but Mr. Goodman greatly favors it. The bearing qualities of the grafts on resistants can be better told in a year or two than at present.

J. Green, Napa.—Total, 7 acres; all in bearing; soil alluvial; vineyard low lying; crop, 11 tons.

A. H. Grossman, Napa.—Total, 60 acres; in bearing, 20 acres; planted to Riparia, 60 acres, 20 acres of which are grafted and bearing and 40 are grafted but not bearing; Alicante Bouschet and Mondeuse have succeeded best; soil rocky and gravelly; vineyard upland; exposure west; crop, 25 tons; cooperage, 15,000 gallons, of which 5,000 is oak and 10,000 is redwood.
Mr. Grossman has made many careful experiments with various resistants during several years. Seven or eight years ago he planted a few hundred each of Riparia, Californica, Rupestris, Lenoir, Elvira, and others. After repeated trials, he has come to the conclusion that the best resistant is the Riparia, and now uses that root. Lenoir does well in places, but for an all-around resistant he prefers the Riparia, thus indorsing the views of the majority of vineyardists who have experimented with resistants. "But," he said, "every vineyardist must find out the variety of vinifera best suited to his soil and location, and graft that on the resistant. One variety may do well in one vineyard and utterly fail in another. That has been my experience. For my own vineyard I much prefer Mondeuse, although Alicante Bouschet does well. Patience, time, and expense are required to find out these things. In conversation with others well able to judge, I think there are not more than 800 acres of resistants in this county, 300 of which, probably, are in bearing. Six years will elapse before the others will be in full bearing."

Joseph Gyte, Napa.—Total, 16 acres; all in bearing; infested by phylloxera, 5 acres, of which 3 acres will last one year more; soil light loam; vineyard upland; exposure southeast; crop, 25 tons.

Henry Hagen, Napa.—Total, 70 acres; in bearing, 40 acres; planted to Riparia, 60 acres, and to Lenoir, 10 acres; of the total, 40 acres are grafted and in bearing, and 30 acres grafted but not bearing; the Sauvignon Vert, Mondeuse, Cabernet, etc., are all doing well on Riparia, and the Burgundy is doing remarkably well on the Lenoir; soil light loam; vineyard upland; exposure west; all European varieties go alike; vines were uprooted as the disease appeared; crop, 77 tons; cooperage, 100,000 gallons, half oak and half redwood.
The grafts were put in resistant stocks when four or five years old. It was found that they did better than when younger. All now bear well. Mr. Hagen is pleased with his success, and favors Riparias. This vineyard, or that portion planted to resistants, is coming along rapidly. Riparia on this reddish, loamy, upland soil does well. The stocks are allowed to get a good growth before they are grafted to European varieties. Mr. Hagen says it is better to wait a year or two longer than some do, in order to let the roots and stock get a good start. Don't graft too deep, and look after the roots, that the scion may not put out, clip them off. He is surprised at the way our grafted vines yield, and is much pleased with success attending grafted resistants. Vineyard was destroyed by phylloxera a few years ago, but resistants put in same ground have continued to flourish.

Harker Bros., Napa.—Total acres, 40; in bearing, 30 acres; soil loam; vineyard mountain; exposure southwest; crop, 38 tons.

J. R. Harris, Napa.—Total, 47 acres; in bearing, 14 acres; in table grapes, 3 acres; soil loam; vineyard mountain; exposure southeast and west; all European varieties succumb alike; crop, 30 tons.
This vineyard is on Atlas Peak. There is no phylloxera in this neighborhood.

Mrs. M. E. Harron, Napa.—Total, 20 acres; all in bearing; infested by phylloxera, 15 acres, all of which will be uprooted in the spring of 1893; acres in Riparia, 5, all of which are grafted to Cabernet and are in bearing; soil loam; vineyard low lying; attacked vines are dug up from year to year; crop, 38 tons.

A. H. Heidhoff, Napa.—Total, 6 acres; in bearing, 4 acres; vineyard mountain; exposure southeast; all European varieties succumb alike; crop, 12 tons.
This is a hill vineyard in the Napa redwoods.

John Hein, Napa.—Total, 18 acres; in bearing, 4 acres; infested by phylloxera, 16 acres; soil loam; vineyard mountain; exposure southeast; no care given attacked vines; crop, 15 tons; cooperage, 20,000 gallons, of which 15,000 is oak and 5,000 redwood.
He will pull up the entire vineyard this season.

P. Heinrich, Napa.—Total, 15 acres; in bearing, 12 acres; will replant 3 acres; soil loam; vineyard low lying; crop, 20 tons.

P. B. Hewlett, Napa.—Total, 40 acres; all in bearing; soil loam; vineyard upland; all European varieties succumb alike; crop, 85 tons.

Mrs. H. M. Howe, Napa.—Total, 7 acres; soil loam; vineyard mountain; exposure south; crop, 18 tons.
This vineyard is on Atlas Peak, thus far exempt from attack.

G. Jaco, Napa.—Total, 5 acres; in bearing, 3½ acres; infested by phylloxera, 4 acres, of which 1 acre is good for only one crop more; soil gravelly; vineyard upland; exposure west; all varieties succumb; crop, 8 tons.
This vineyard is fast going.

P. Jordon, Napa.—Total, 50 acres; in bearing, 20 acres; planted to Riparia, 30 acres; to Lenoir, 20 acres; of resistants, 25 acres are grafted and bearing, and 25 are grafted but not bearing. All grafts succeed alike; Sweetwater Riesling has proved most resistant; crop, 44 tons; stock of wine on hand, 3,000 gallons; cooperage, 10,000 gallons, of which 3,000 is oak and 7,000 is redwood.
Some Arizonica and Californica were experimented with, but proved unsatisfactory. Riparia is considered best, although Lenoir does very well. Some vineyards in this vicinity have been entirely destroyed.

J. R. S. Kingley, Napa.—Total, 125 acres; in bearing, 100 acres; planted to resistants, 125 acres of different varieties; soil loamy; vineyard upland; exposure south and west; crop, 175 tons.
This vineyard is on the Simonton Estate. Resistant stocks were planted by Professor Husmann eight or ten years ago. It is rented now of the third owner since that time, so it is hard to tell about the amount of the different varieties of resistants. All grafts seem to be doing well, but Riparia is the favorite in this neighborhood.

J. Klam, Napa.—Total, 20 acres; in bearing, 16 acres; infested by phylloxera, 2 acres; soil loam; vineyard upland; all varieties succumb alike; crop, 45 tons.
Many vineyards are infested in this locality.

J. F. Knief, Napa.—Total, 20 acres; in bearing, 10 acres; will replant, 5 acres; planted to Riparia, 10 acres, and to Rupestris, 10 acres; acres grafted and bearing, 10; grafted but not yet bearing, 5 acres; not yet grafted, 5 acres; soil rocky and loamy hillside; vineyard upland; exposure southwest; crop, 25 tons; cooperage, 20,000 gallons, of which 6,000 is oak and 14,000 redwood.
Mr. Knief does not like Zinfandel on resistant stocks. Carignan do well, and also Mataro. He favors Rupestris as a resistant, as the Riparia roots are too near the surface. The Rupestris does not root so easily, but has been with him a more satisfactory stock, all things considered.

O. L. Krenz, Napa.—Total, 20 acres; in bearing, 10 acres; infested by phylloxera, 15 acres; soil light loam; vineyard low lying; vineyard neglected; crop, 15 tons.
This vineyard will be totally uprooted this winter.

N. Lang, Napa.—Total, 20 acres; all in bearing; infested by phylloxera, 10 acres, of which 2 acres are good for only one crop more; soil gravelly; vineyard low lying; crop, 50 tons.

G. W. May, Napa.—Total, 20 acres; all in bearing; infested by phylloxera, 5 acres, of which 3 acres will last one year only; soil rocky and gravelly; vineyard upland; crop, 50 tons.

A. McFarland, Napa.—Total, 17 acres; all in bearing; soil heavy loam; vineyard low lying; all attacked vines succumb alike; crop, 20 tons.

Same, Napa.—Total, 10 acres; in bearing, 10 acres; infested by phylloxera, 3 acres, of which 1 acre will last only one year; soil reddish loam; vineyard upland; crop, 20 tons.

P. Meyer, Napa.—Total, 20 acres; all in bearing; infested by phylloxera, 5 acres, of which 1 acre is good for only one crop more; soil loam; vineyard low lying; crop, 54 tons.

Drury Melone, Napa.—Total, 13 acres; in bearing, 5 acres; will replant a few vines; planted to Riparia, 13 acres, of which 5 are grafted and bearing and 8 are grafted and not bearing; Mondeuse and Sauvignon Vert grafts do well; soil loam; vineyard low lying; crop, 9 tons.

Am not much in favor of extended replanting, as the outlook is poor. Riparia is favored, and consider it the only salvation of vineyardists.

Mrs. J. M. Meridith, Napa.—Total, 15 acres; all in bearing; will replant 3 acres; infested by phylloxera, 1 acre; soil gravelly; vineyard low lying; all European varieties succumb alike; have used sulphate of iron, 1 pound to 10 gallons of water, for attacked vines, applied to vines in the spring when the ground is wet; crop, 25 tons.

The effect of sulphate of iron wash could be seen for a year or two, but do not know if the benefit will be permanent. Shall continue to use this application, but do not know as it will fully restore the diseased vines.

G. Migliavacca, Napa.—Cooperage (estimated), 450,000 gallons, of which 50,000 is oak and 400,000 redwood.

Estate of John F. Miller (Mrs. Clover), Napa.—Total, 50 acres; in bearing, 35 acres; will replant about 5 acres; infested by phylloxera, 5 acres, of which 3 are good for only one year; planted to Riparia, 40 acres, of which 35 are grafted and in bearing and 5 acres grafted but not bearing; the Cabernet Sauvignon and Carignan grafts have done well, but the Burgundy has not been as successful; soil loam; vineyard low lying; the attacked vines have been dug out from year to year; crop, 52 tons.

The resistants at this vineyard have done well, and there is every indication of their being a continued success. The Riparia is a favorite stock.

Parker Estate, Napa.—Total, 50 acres; in bearing, 40 acres; infested by phylloxera, 25 acres, of which 20 acres are badly eaten and will last only one year more; soil heavy loam; vineyard low lying; no pains taken with attacked vines; crop, 90 tons.

This vineyard is going very rapidly. Two years ago the phylloxera commenced working in 75 acres of thrifty vines. It is very doubtful if any care is given the vineyard after 1893. This is only one of many vineyards in the lower valley that will be entirely destroyed in a year or two.

Mrs. Penny, Napa.—Total, 10 acres; all in bearing; infested by phylloxera, 3 acres, of which 2 acres will last but a year more; soil loam; vineyard low lying; crop, 25 tons.

Dr. M. B. Pond, Napa.—Total, 30 acres; in bearing, 20 acres; planted to resistants, 10 acres, all bearing, of which 4 are in Riparia, 3 Rupestris, and 3 Lenoir; soil dark and light loam; vineyard mountain; exposure north and east; crop, 40 tons; cooperage, 16,000 gallons, of which 1,000 is oak and 15,000 redwood.

Vineyard is 1,700 feet above tidewater at Napa, and is among the redwoods. It is growing finely. The resistants have succeeded well, and this year a box of grapes from every three or four vines has been gathered, one year from the grafting. Riparia is in the most favor. Rupestris is slower, and the Lenoir is least esteemed as a grafting stock.

A. T. Prentiss, Napa.—Total, 25 acres; all in bearing; infested by phylloxera, 5 acres, of which 1 acre is good for only one crop more; soil gravelly; vineyard upland; crop, 45 tons.

P. Priet, Napa.—Total, 80 acres; all in bearing; soil loam; vineyard upland; crop, 200 tons; cooperage, 75,000 gallons, of which 25,000 is oak and 50,000 redwood.

—— *Reed, Napa.*—Total, 36 acres; in bearing 22 acres; will replant 3 acres; planted to Riparia, 36 acres, of which 22 acres are grafted and 14 are grafted but not bearing; Cabernet Sauvignon, St. Macaire, and Pinot grafts succeed best; soil deep loam; vineyard upland; exposure east and south; crop, 11 tons.

Planted my first Riparia several years ago. When I set them out I had 1,000 vines in the vineyard not on resistant roots. Every one of them long since died, being killed by phylloxera. I have not noticed a single resistant vine that appears unhealthy. I grafted at two years old. The Riparia has great vitality. When I planted the vineyard I set it out solid; afterwards I took out every twenty-fifth row. I made one mistake—or rather the grafters did. The grafts placed too deep all died.

E. A. Rety, Napa.—Total, 45 acres; in bearing, 30 acres; will replant 3 acres; infested by phylloxera, 10 acres, of which half is good for only one crop more; planted to Riparia, 5 acres, of which 3 are grafted and in bearing, and 2 grafted but not bearing; Mataro, Cabernet, and Grenache have all done well on resistants; soil loam; vineyard mountain; exposure northeast; vines are rooted out as soon as attacked; crop, 60 tons; cooperage, 15,000 gallons, all redwood.

Charles Robinson, Napa.—Total, 60 acres; in bearing, 40 acres; will replant 5 acres; infested by phylloxera, 10 acres, half of which is good for only one crop more; planted to resistants, 30 acres, all grafted and in bearing, and of which 25 acres are in Riparia and

5 acres in Lenoir; all grafts have done well on both stocks; Malvoisie has done well in resisting phylloxera among European varieties; crop, 80 tons; cooperage, 30,000 gallons of which 15,000 is oak and 15,000 redwood.

Mrs. M. J. Rose, Napa.—Total, 15 acres; all in bearing; soil loam; vineyard mountain; crop, 42 tons.

Jas. Salmini, Napa.—Total, 15 acres; in bearing, 12 acres; infested by phylloxera, acres, of which 2 acres are good for only one crop more; soil rocky loam; vineyard upland; exposure west; Mataro and Carignan have resisted the phylloxera well; crop, 25 tons.

J. L. Shearer, Napa.—Total, 12 acres; all in bearing; soil gravelly; vineyard low lying; crop, 30 tons.
This is one of the few healthy vineyards in this vicinity.

B. B. Smith, Napa.—Total, 70 acres; will replant 5 acres; infested by phylloxera, 5 acres of which 2 will bear but one crop more; planted to Riparia, 3 acres, none of which is grafted; soil loam; vineyard upland; exposure southwest; no efforts made to check the disease; crop, 35 tons.

John T. Smith, Napa.—Total, 10 acres; in bearing, 8 acres; infested by phylloxera, acres, of which half will bear but one more crop; soil loam; vineyard upland; exposure southeast; Zinfandel has resisted fairly well; crop, 20 tons.

D. R. Sommers, Napa.—Total, 6 acres; in bearing, 3 acres; infested by phylloxera, acres, all of which will be dug up in the spring of 1893; soil loam; vineyard low lying no pains taken with attacked vines; crop, 7 tons.

John A. Stanly, Napa.—Total, 125 acres; in full bearing, 80 acres; planted to resistants 125 acres, of which 118 are in Riparia and 7 in Lenoir; of the 125 acres, 90 are grafted and in partial bearing, and 35 acres not yet grafted. All varieties that have been grafted to Riparia have succeeded; no Lenoirs grafted; soil varied; vineyard upland (rolling low hills); exposure every direction; crop about two thirds.
This vineyard is planted to red wine varieties. Judge Stanly was probably the first person to introduce resistant vines into this county, in 1882. He planted them against the judgment of many vineyardists. They have succeeded well. "The only vine I think absolutely resistant is Riparia. I am well satisfied with my resistants. I would never plant anything else. Since I planted my first resistants, within three miles of my vineyard, 500 acres have been planted to vines and eaten up by phylloxera. My vineyard is flourishing. Grafts should not be put in deep; quite near the surface is best. Hill up about grafts in October. Many grafts have failed because put in too deep." This vineyard demonstrates the adaptability of Riparia to our vineyards as a resistant.

L. S. Starkweather, Napa.—Total, 45 acres; in bearing, 35 acres; infested by phylloxera, 8 acres, half of which will bear but one more crop; soil gravelly loam; vineyard low lying; crop, 40 tons.

C. Steiffel, Napa.—Total, 15 acres; in bearing, 10 acres; infested by phylloxera, 7 acres, of which 4 acres will bear but one crop more; soil loam; vineyard upland; exposure east; no special care given attacked vines; crop, 40 tons.

Ernest Streich, Napa.—Total, 200 acres; in bearing, 10 acres; planted to Riparia, 190 acres, some of which are grafted and some not grafted; soil loam; vineyard mountain; exposure southeast; crop, 30 tons; cooperage, 5,000 gallons, of which 2,000 is oak and 3,000 redwood.
The grafts thus far are growing well. This vineyard is in the Napa redwoods.

S. Strong, Napa.—Total, 15 acres; in bearing, 12 acres; infested by phylloxera, 10 acres, of which 3 acres will bear but one crop more; soil loam; vineyard low lying; exposure east; not much care given attacked vines; crop, 32 tons.

J. C. Sullivan, Napa.—Total, 9 acres; in bearing, 4 acres; will replant 6 acres; infested by phylloxera, 6 acres, of which 2 acres will bear but one crop more; planted to Riparia, 3 acres, of which 2 acres are grafted and in bearing, and 1 acre grafted but not yet bearing; Zinfandel and Golden Chasselas have succeeded well; soil gravelly loam; vineyard upland; exposure west and southeast; vines uprooted when diseased; Zinfandel has resisted fairly well; crop, 4 tons.
Lenoir, as a stock, is in poor favor in this vicinity.

Henry Tasche, Napa.—Total, 5 acres; all in bearing; soil gravelly; vineyard upland; crop, 14 tons.

Thomas Tracy, Napa.—Total, 10 acres; all in bearing; soil loam; vineyard low lying; crop, 28 tons.

W. W. Thompson, Napa.—Total, 107 acres; all in bearing; infested by phylloxera, 15 acres, of which 5 acres will bear but one crop more; planted to Riparia, 5 acres, all of which are grafted and in bearing; all varieties grafted have succeeded; soil gravelly loam; vineyard upland; exposure west; Tokay and Zinfandel have resisted fairly well; crop, 472 tons.
About 6 or 7 acres will be pulled out this winter.

Frank Verroni, Napa.—Total, 14 acres; all in bearing; soil gravelly and rocky; vineyard upland; crop, 25 tons.

J. Vopt, Napa.—Total, 60 acres; all in bearing; soil loam; vineyard mountain; exposure west and south; crop, 100 tons; cooperage, 50,000 gallons, of which 10,000 is oak and 40,000 redwood.
This vineyard is on the extreme ridge of hills dividing Napa from Wooden Valley.

John T. Ward, Napa.—Total, 15 acres; in bearing, 10 acres; infested by phylloxera, 10 acres, of which 5 acres will bear but one more crop; soil light loam; vineyard upland; no special care given attacked vines; crop, 4 tons.
This vineyard is fast disappearing.

W. Weeks, Napa.—Total, 27 acres; in bearing, 20 acres; infested by phylloxera, 15 acres, of which 6 will bear but one crop more; soil gravelly loam; vineyard low lying; crop, 45 tons.

E. Yates, Napa.—Total, 10 acres; all in bearing; infested by phylloxera, 5 acres, of which 1 acre will bear but one crop more; soil loam; vineyard low lying; crop, 25 tons.
The phylloxera is working gradually, and some vineyards in this vicinity have been entirely destroyed.

Mrs. E. G. Young, Napa.—Total, 40 acres; in bearing, 28 acres; infested by phylloxera, 20 acres, of which 10 acres will bear but one crop more; soil shading to adobe; no special care given attacked vines; crop, 25 tons.
The vines in the vineyard are fast going.

YOUNTVILLE DISTRICT.

John Benson, Oakville.—Total, 35 acres; in bearing, 30 acres; will replant 5 acres; infested by phylloxera, 10 acres, all to be uprooted; planted to Riparia, 25 acres, which is grafted to Semillon, Mondeuse, Cabernet Franc, and all succeed about alike; soil loam bordering on adobe; vineyard low lying; European varieties most resistant, Zinfandel and Burger; vineyard replanted as vines become diseased; crop, 50 tons; cooperage, 90,000 gallons, of which 5,000 is oak and 85,000 redwood.

W. P. Bolz, Oakville.—Total, 15 acres; in bearing, 12 acres; all will be dug up; soil gravelly loam; vineyard upland; all European varieties succumb alike; crop, 35 tons.

W. T. Bradley, Oakville.—Total, 25 acres; all in bearing; infested by phylloxera, 12 acres, of which 4 acres are good for only one crop more; soil gravelly loam; vineyard low lying; European varieties all succumb alike; crop, 43 tons.

B. Bradshaw, Oakville.—Total, 5 acres; in bearing, 4 acres; infested by phylloxera, 4 acres, of which 2 acres are good for only one crop more; soil gravelly; vineyard upland; exposure northwest; European varieties all succumb alike; crop, 8 tons. Vineyard will be gone in two years.

George Brainard, Oakville.—Total, 50 acres; in bearing, 48 acres; infested by phylloxera. 5 acres, of which 2 acres are good for only one crop more; vineyard low lying; all European varieties succumb alike; crop, 14 tons.

Brun & Chaix, Oakville.—Total, 115 acres; in bearing, 113 acres; will plant 15 or 20 acres; soil loam; vineyard low lying and mountain; exposure south; crop, 350 tons; cooperage, 300,000 gallons at Howell Mountain and 150,000 in valley at Oakville, mostly redwood. One vineyard and cellar is on Howell Mountain. Have escaped phylloxera so far, but expect it before long.

Duncan Campbell, Oakville.—Total, 10 acres; in bearing, 6 acres; infested by phylloxera, 5 acres, of which 2 acres are good for only one crop more; soil loam; vineyard upland; exposure east; all European varieties succumb alike; crop, 12 tons. Vineyard going fast.

Thomas Dwyer, Oakville.—Total, 10 acres; all in bearing; infested by phylloxera, 2 acres, of which 1 acre is good for only one crop more; soil loam; vineyard low lying; crop, 6 tons.

H. W. Crabb, Oakville.—Total, 120 acres; in bearing, 90 acres; infested by phylloxera, 20 acres; planted to resistants, 100 acres, of which 70 are Riparia and 30 Lenoir, and all of which are doing well; soil loam; vineyard low lying; exposure south and east; Tokay has proved most resistant; vines dug out as soon as diseased; crop, 100 tons; cooperage, 650,-000 gallons, all of which is redwood.
This is one of the several vineyards in this vicinity that were very flourishing four years ago, but have rapidly decayed. The destruction was surprisingly rapid and very discouraging. Mr. Crabb is planting out resistants year by year, to a considerable extent, both Lenoir and Riparia, the former on the high drier soil, the latter on the lower, stiffer land. Success seems to attend the growth of resistants. Experience in this vicinity shows plainly that resistants (cuttings or rooted vines) should be planted early in the season, especially if the season should prove to be a dry one. In two or three years more definite views can be given as to bearing of resistants.

Davis Estate, Oakville.—Total, 55 acres; in bearing, 50 acres; infested by phylloxera, 15 acres, of which 6 acres are good for only one crop more; soil gravelly; vineyard low lying; crop, 120 tons; cooperage, 40,000 gallons, all of which is redwood.

F. Delmont, Oakville.—Total, 10 acres; all in bearing; infested by phylloxera, 5 acres, of which 1 acre is good for one year more; soil gravelly; vineyard low lying; crop, 22 tons.

Dietrich Bros., Oakville.—Total, 15 acres; all in bearing; planted to Riparia, 2 acres, which are grafted and bearing; vineyard upland; exposure east; Tokay and Malvoisie have proved most resistant; crop, 30 tons.

D. Downey, Oakville.—Total, 46 acres; in bearing, 40 acres; infested by phylloxera, 16 acres, of which 10 acres are good for only one crop more; soil loam; vineyard low lying; all European varieties succumb alike; diseased vines have received no care; crop, 105 tons; stock of wine on hand, 10,000 gallons; cooperage, 30,000 gallons, of which 1,000 is oak and 29,000 redwood.

A. Dwyer, Oakville.—Total, 30 acres; in bearing, 23 acres; infested by phylloxera, 20 acres, of which 10 are good for only one crop more; soil gravelly loam: vineyard upland; exposure southwest; all European varieties succumb alike; diseased varieties have received no special care; crop, 50 tons.

John Forrester, Oakville.—Total, 6 acres; in bearing, 5 acres; infested by phylloxera, 4 acres, of which 2 acres are good for only one crop more; soil loam; vineyard low lying; all European varieties succumb alike; crop, 15 tons.

C. H. Hill, Oakville.—Total, 6 acres; in bearing, 5 acres; very little infested by phylloxera; soil loam; vineyard upland; exposure southeast; all European varieties succumb alike; crop, 24 tons.

P. G. Hottle, Oakville.—Total, 20 acres; in bearing, 15 acres; infested by phylloxera, 10 acres, of which 2 acres are good for only one crop more; crop, 30 tons. Vineyard is going fast.

A. Jeanmonod, Oakville.—Total, 20 acres; all in bearing; infested by phylloxera, 5 acres, of which 1 acre is good for only one crop more; soil gravelly; vineyard low lying; all European varieties succumb alike; crop, 32 tons; cooperage, 60,000 gallons, of which 10,000 is oak and 50,000 is redwood.

T. Julian, Oakville.—Total, 12 acres; in bearing, 10 acres; infested by phylloxera, 2 acres, of which 1 acre is good for only one crop more; planted to Riparia, 2 acres; soil clayey loam; vineyard mountain; exposure southeast; all European varieties succumb alike; crop, 40 tons.

M. Kemper, Oakville.—Total, 60 acres; in bearing, 50 acres; infested by phylloxera, 20 acres, of which 5 acres are good for only one crop more; soil loam; vineyard low lying; crop, 90 tons.

Jos. Kidd, Oakville.—Total, 40 acres; in bearing, 30 acres; soil heavy loam; vineyard low lying; crop, 60 tons.

W. Locker, Oakville.—Total, 25 acres, all of which are in bearing; infested by phylloxera, 10 acres, of which 3 acres are good for only one crop more; soil gravelly; vineyard low lying; crop, 60 tons; cooperage, 20,000 gallons, of which 5,000 is oak and 15,000 redwood.

J. J. McIntyre, Oakville.—Total, 20 acres, all of which are in bearing; infested by phylloxera, 8 acres, of which 3 acres are good for only one year more; soil loam; vineyard low lying; all European varieties succumb alike; crop, 75 tons.

C. Minion, Oakville.—Total, 10 acres; in bearing, 8 acres; infested by phylloxera, 3 acres, of which 2 acres are good for only one crop more; soil loamy; vineyard upland; exposure southeast; crop, 30 tons.

A. Mono, Oakville.—Total, 20 acres; in bearing, 10 acres; will replant 10 acres; infested by phylloxera, 15 acres, of which 8 acres are good for only one crop more; planted to Riparia, 10 acres, of which 5 acres are in bearing; grafted Bouschet, which is doing very well; soil loamy and gravelly; vineyard low lying; Tokays proved most resistant; much care has been taken to dig out as soon as possible and replant; crop, 27 tons; cooperage, 40,000 gallons, of which 5,000 is oak and 35,000 redwood.
Bouschet grafts do exceedingly well. One graft, 8 months old, on a 2-year old resistant Riparia root, yielded 8 pounds.

A. C. Montgomery, Oakville.—Total, 60 acres; in bearing, 50 acres; infested by phylloxera, 40 acres, of which 20 acres are good for only one crop more; soil loam; vineyard low lying; all European varieties succumb alike; crop, 132 tons.

A. Reinder, Oakville.—Total, 5 acres; in bearing, 4 acres; nearly all infested by phylloxera; 2 acres are good for only one crop more; soil loam; vineyard upland; exposure east; crop, 8 tons.
This is one of the several vineyards on the hills to the west of Oakville. Phylloxera is as destructive there as in any place in the lower lands. Vineyards are fast disappearing, and the outlook discourages many vineyardists, especially those having small holdings.

R. Stice, Oakville.—Total, 40 acres; in bearing, 30 acres; infested by phylloxera, 25 acres, of which 8 acres will be good for only one crop more; vineyard upland; exposure west; all European varieties succumb alike; diseased vines have received little care; crop, 63 tons.

A. Wright, Oakville.—Total, 10 acres; in bearing, 8 acres; infested by phylloxera, 3 acres; of which 1 acre is good for only one crop more; soil loam; vineyard upland; exposure east; Tokay and Zinfandel have proved most resistant of European vines; crop, 25 tons.

C. J. Beerstecher, Rutherford.—Total, 100 acres; in bearing, 80 acres; infested by phylloxera, 15 acres, of which 5 acres are good for only one crop more; soil loam; vineyard mountain; crop, 210 tons; cooperage, 75,000 gallons, of which 5,000 is oak and 70,000 is redwood.

H. Lang, Rutherford.—Total, 20 acres; in bearing, 15 acres; infested by phylloxera, 10 acres, of which 3 acres will be good for only one crop more; soil gravelly; vineyard low lying; crop, 25 tons; cooperage, 80,000 gallons, of which 5,000 gallons is oak and ;75,000 is redwood.

Chas. Menneger, Rutherford.—Total, 8 acres; all in bearing; infested by phylloxera, 3 acres, of which 1 acre is good for only one crop more; soil gravelly loam; vineyard low lying; crop, 20 tons.

A. Montgomery, Rutherford.—Total, 68 acres; in bearing, 60 acres; infested by phylloxera, 20 acres, of which 10 acres are good for only one crop more; soil gravelly; vineyard low lying; all European varieties succumb alike; diseased vines have received no special treatment; crop, 75 tons.

J. M. Morton, Rutherford.—Total, 20 acres; all in bearing; planted to Riparia, 7 acres, not grafted; soil gravelly; vineyard low lying; crop, 60 tons; cooperage, 14,000 gallons, all of which is redwood.

Capt. G. Niebaum, Rutherford.—Total, 300 acres; in bearing, 250 acres; will replant considerable; planted to Riparia, 50 acres, of which 20 acres are grafted and not bearing and 30 acres are not grafted; all grafts are doing well; soil gravelly loam; vineyard low lying and upland; crop, 408 tons; cooperage, 350,000 gallons, of which 100,000 is oak and 250,000 is redwood.
Considerable pains have been taken in this vineyard with resistants. Riparia are most in favor; they have done well and·given satisfaction. Will continue to replant. Phylloxera is working in the old European vines and a considerable amount will be dug up and replanted each year. The grafted vines are flourishing and doing well.

William Porter, Rutherford.—Total, 50 acres; all in bearing; infested by phylloxera, 10 acres, of which 2 acres are good for only one crop more; soil gravelly; vineyard low lying; crop, 115 tons.

Mrs. Rutherford, Rutherford.—Total, 60 acres; in bearing, 55 acres; infested by phylloxera, 5 acres; soil gravelly loam; vineyard low lying; Golden Chasselas and Tokay have proved most resistant; crop, 125 tons; cooperage, 50,000 gallons, of which 10,000 is oak and 40,000 is redwood.
Very little phylloxera.

N. Sawyer, Rutherford.—Total, 30 acres; all in bearing; infested by phylloxera, 10 acres, of which 3 acres are good for only one crop more; soil gravelly loam; vineyard low lying; crop, 75 tons.

C. E. Smith, Rutherford.—Total, 5 acres; in bearing, 3 acres; soil loam; vineyard upland; exposure west; all European varieties succumb alike; crop, nothing to speak of; cooperage, 30,000 gallons, all of which is redwood.
The vines are going fast.

Chas. Thompson, Rutherford.—Total, 40 acres; all in bearing; planted to Riparia, 8 acres; all grafted and not bearing; soil gravelly; vineyard low lying; crop, 75 tons.
Resistants grafted to Tokays have not proved entirely successful, because of failure to remove the rootlets from the scions; they were grafted too deep.

B. Wagnon, Rutherford.—Total, 27 acres; in bearing, 24 acres; infested by phylloxera, 10 acres, of which 3 acres are good for only one crop more; soil gravelly; vineyard low lying; all European varieties succumb alike; crop, 35 tons.

A. Borel & Co., Yountville (Groezinger Vineyard).—Total, 125 acres; in bearing, 65 acres; will replant 25 acres; infested by phylloxera, 42 acres, 30 of which will bear but one crop more; planted to resistants, 83 acres, of which 52 are in Riparia, 30 in Californica, 1,150 vines of Lenoir, and a few Rupestris vines; of these resistants, 30 acres are grafted and bearing, 12 acres grafted but not bearing, and 41 acres not yet grafted; on Riparia all varieties did well, and the same is true with the few Rupestris vines tried; Petite Syrah has done well on Lenoir, but all others have failed, while on Californica·and Arizonica all varieties did well for the first two or three years, and then all failed; soil is shallow, and on the low land heavy, cold, and wet; one fourth of the vineyard is upland, and the soil is deep and rich; exposure northeast, north, and east; Tokay and Lenoir have resisted well; attacked vines have been treated with all known and proposed remedies; crop, 152 tons; cooperage, 320,000 gallons, of which 210,000 is oak and 110,000 redwood.
Mr. Greninger, the Superintendent, has experimented for the past eight years with all the different varieties of resistant vines, and finds that the Lenoir and Californica will not withstand the attack of the phylloxera. Rupestris, Arizonica, Herbemont, and others did fairly well in certain places only. Riparia has done the best on all kinds of soil, and has succeeded best with different kinds and varieties of grafts. The original vineyard was of 402 acres, with 83 varieties of grapes. All the hill vineyard is now being abandoned, on account of being too expensive to care for and work.

E. Breseind, Yountville.—Total, 30 acres; in bearing, 25 acres; will replant 5 acres; infested by phylloxera, 5 acres, of which 2 acres are good for only one crop more; soil loam; vineyard low lying; exposure northwest; all European varieties succumb alike; crop, 45 tons; cooperage, 15,000 gallons, all of which is oak.

M. Eckmyer, Yountville.—Total, 35 acres; in bearing, 17 acres; infested by phylloxera, 20 acres, of which 10 acres will be good for only one crop more; soil gravelly loam; vineyard upland; exposure east; all European varieties succumb alike; crop, 16 tons.
Vineyards in this vicinity are fast decaying.

Fred. Ellis, Yountville.—Total, 15 acres; in bearing, 8 acres; will replant 2 acres; planted to Riparia, 10 acres, half grafted and not bearing, and half not yet grafted; crop, 48 tons. There are some diseased vines, which will all come up this winter.

J. W. Fawver, Yountville.—Total, 30 acres; in bearing, 20 acres; soil loam; vineyard low lying; all European varieties succumb alike; the diseased vines have been neglected; crop, 60 tons.
This vineyard four years ago was most flourishing, but now is five sixths gone, and all vines will be dug out next spring. This is very discouraging. Several vineyards in this vicinity are entirely gone.

Mrs. Fluger, Yountville.—Total, 20 acres; in bearing, 15 acres; infested by phylloxera, 4 acres, of which 2 acres are good for only one crop more; soil gravelly loam; vineyard upland; exposure east; all European varieties succumb alike; diseased vines have received little care; crop, 4 tons.

A. Franco, Yountville.—Total, 30 acres; infested by phylloxera, 5 acres; soil loam; vineyard upland; exposure northeast; all European varieties succumb alike; diseased vines have received no special care; crop, 50 tons.

Fred. Frast, Yountville.—Total, 15 acres; in bearing, 11 acres; planted to Riparia, 4 acres; half grafted but not bearing, and half not yet grafted; soil loam; vineyard low lying; crop, 50 tons.

Col. J. D. Frye, Yountville.—Total, 70 acres; in bearing, 30 acres; will replant several acres; planted to Riparia, 20 acres, not yet grafted; soil gravelly; vineyard upland; exposure east; all European varieties succumb the same; crop, 40 tons; cooperage, 110,000 gallons, of which 50,000 is oak and 60,000 is redwood.
Riparia has proved the best resistant. It is difficult to ascertain definitely the acreage planted, for resistants are planted in spots. The original vineyard is going fast. The vines on light soil go first, and then those on damp soil. In a vineyard not far from this one the manager thinks phylloxera attacks vines quicker that are over underground watercourses.

Levi George, Yountville.—Total, 18 acres; in bearing, 15 acres; infested by phylloxera, 5 acres, of which 3 will be good for only one crop more; soil loam; vineyard low lying; exposure southwest; all European vines succumb alike; the vines have been dug out as soon as decayed; crop, 125 tons.

Mrs. Gibbs, Yountville.—Total, 30 acres; in bearing, 28 acres; very little has been infested by phylloxera; vineyard low lying; all European varieties succumb alike; no extra care has been given to the attacked vineyards; crop, 65 tons.

J. Hahn, Yountville.—Total, 90 acres; in bearing, 10 acres; infested by phylloxera, about 10 acres, all of which will be uprooted this winter; planted to Riparia, 85 acres, of which 5 are grafted and in bearing, 5 acres are grafted and not bearing, and 75 not yet grafted; Mondeuse graft has succeeded best; soil loam; vineyard low lying and upland; exposure east; Malvoisie and Tokay have proved most resistant; the attacked vines have been dug up soon after infested; crop, 27 tons.
Great pains have been taken with resistants in this vineyard, and the grafts are growing well, and will yield well from appearances. Californicas (resistant) are regarded here as too soft to be used; Riparia does best in this vicinity.

A. Hansen, Yountville.—Total, 15 acres; all in bearing; soil loam; vineyard low lying; crop, 22 tons.

Ex-Governor Johnson, Yountville.—Total, 15 acres; in bearing, 10 acres; infested by phylloxera, 5 acres, of which 3 acres are good for only one crop more; soil gravelly loam; vineyard upland; exposure east; all European varieties succumb alike; crop, 38 tons.

W. L. Johnson, Yountville.—Total, 10 acres; in bearing, 8 acres; infested by phylloxera, 5 acres, of which 2 acres are good for only one crop more; soil gravelly loam; vineyard upland; exposure west; all European varieties succumb alike; not much care has been given the attacked vineyards; crop, 18 tons.
This vineyard will be dug up in a year or so.

W. P. Kelly, Yountville.—Total, 15 acres; in bearing, 10 acres; infested by phylloxera, 8 acres, of which 4 acres are good for only one crop more; soil gravelly; vineyard low lying; exposure northwest; all European varieties succumb alike; crop, 30 acres.

C. Lambert, Yountville.—Total, 20 acres; in bearing, 10 acres; infested by phylloxera, 15 acres; of which 15 acres are good for only one crop more; soil gravelly; vineyard upland; exposure west; all European varieties succumb alike; crop, 10 tons.
This vineyard is going fast.

C. L. Larue, Yountville.—Total, 110 acres; in bearing, 45 acres; will replant 20 acres; infested by phylloxera, 30 acres, of which 5 are good for only one crop more; planted to

Riparia, 65 acres, and to Californica, 5 acres; of which 25 acres are grafted and in bearing, 5 acres are grafted and not bearing, and 40 acres are not yet grafted. The grafts Mondeuse, Burgundy, Semillon, and Bouschet have succeeded alike; soil gravelly loam; vineyard low lying; exposure east; of the European varieties, Malvoisie, Zinfandel, and Chasselas have proved about equally resistant; great care has been taken to replant resistants as soon as vines are attacked; crop, 220 tons.

Mr. Larue has given much time and close attention to the planting of resistants, and has met with considerable success. Neither Lenoir nor Californica are favored here. The resistants in bearing do well and promise good results. Mr. Larue is satisfied that Riparia will do exceedingly well, but can tell more in the course of a year or two. They seem to give general satisfaction as far as he has seen, and he thinks this is the only way to preserve our vineyards, and advises planting them, for they have proved a very good resistant. It is doubtful if there is any better or as good. Rupestris and Californicas are of not much account. We evidently have to choose between Riparia and Lenoir, and the former has been found to stand the test, but the latter will fail in some situations.

Mrs. Lycan, Yountville.—Total, 5 acres; in bearing, 4 acres; infested by phylloxera, 4 acres, of which 1 acre is good for only one crop more; soil loam; vineyard low lying; all European varieties succumb alike; the attacked vines have received no care; crop, 10 tons. This is one of the many vineyards in this vicinity that are going fast.

L. H. McGeorge, Yountville.—Total, 10 acres; in bearing, 9 acres; infested by phylloxera, 2 acres, of which 1 acre is good for only one crop more; soil loam; vineyard upland; exposure east; all European varieties succumb alike; attacked vines have been neglected; crop, 20 tons.

Jacob Metz, Yountville.—Total, 15 acres; in bearing, 12 acres; infested by phylloxera, 7 acres, of which 2 acres are good for only one crop more; soil loam; vineyard low lying; crop, 30 tons.

Mrs. Meyers, Yountville.—Total, 75 acres; in bearing, 60 acres; infested by phylloxera, 15 to 20 acres, of which 8 acres are good for only one crop more; crop, 80 tons; cooperage, 60,000 gallons, of which 5,000 is oak and 55,000 is redwood. This vineyard is going fast. It is very uncertain how long these infested vineyards will last, but to all appearances not more than three years.

Frank Morris, Yountville.—Total, 10 acres; in bearing, 8 acres; infested by phylloxera, 10 acres, of which 5 acres are good for only one crop more; soil gravelly; vineyard upland; exposure northwest; all European varieties succumb alike; attacked vines have received little care; crop, 15 tons. This vineyard is going fast.

Nauer Bros., Yountville.—Total, 25 acres; in bearing, 24 acres; infested by phylloxera, 4 acres, of which 2 acres are good for only one crop more; soil gravelly loam; vineyard low lying; all European varieties succumb alike; attacked vines have received no special care; crop, 68 tons.

William Nunn, Yountville.—Total, 30 acres; in bearing, 28 acres; infested by phylloxera, 5 acres, of which 1 acre is good for only one year; soil gravelly; vineyard upland; Zinfandel has proved most resistant; crop, 58 tons.

J. Ohl, Yountville.—Total, 22 acres; in bearing, 10 acres; will replant 25 acres; planted to Riparia, 12 acres, which are not yet grafted; soil rocky; vineyard upland; exposure west; Burger and Zinfandel have proved most resistant; crop, 15 tons.

J. R. Pedlar, Yountville.—Total, 12 acres; in bearing, 8 acres; infested by phylloxera, 10 acres, of which 3 acres are good for only one crop more; soil gravelly loam; vineyard upland; exposure east; all European varieties succumb alike; crop, 20 tons.

M. Pedro, Yountville.—Total, 10 acres; in bearing, 5 acres; infested by phylloxera, 5 acres, of which 2 acres are good for only one crop more; planted to Riparia, 5 acres, which are not grafted; soil reddish light loam; vineyard upland; exposure west; all European varieties succumb alike; attacked vines receive no special treatment; crop, 10 tons. This vineyard is going fast. Mr. Pedro finds it far more profitable to sell the cuttings from his resistant vines than to graft them.

W. T. Ross, Yountville.—Total, 20 acres; in bearing, 12 acres; infested by phylloxera, 10 acres, of which 5 acres are good for only one crop more; soil loam; vineyard upland; exposure west; all European varieties succumb alike; crop, 16 tons. This vineyard is going very fast. It will last only two or three years.

B. Saffold, Yountville.—Total, 10 acres; in bearing, 5 acres; infested by phylloxera, 5 acres, of which 2 acres are good for only one year more; soil loam; vineyard upland; exposure east; crop, 38 tons.

Mrs. Schofield, Yountville.—Total, 12 acres; all in bearing; soil loam; vineyard low lying; exposure southwest; all European varieties succumb alike; crop, 50 tons.

C. Stiefl, Yountville.—Total, 12 acres; all in bearing; infested by phylloxera, 6 acres, 2 of which will bear but one crop more; soil loam; vineyard low lying; crop, 35 tons.

H. Tiederman, Yountville.—Total, 11 acres; in bearing, 10 acres; soil black loam; vineyard low lying; exposure southeast; crop, 35 tons.

Mrs. Van Winkle, Yountville.—Total, 15 acres; in bearing, 5 acres; infested by phylloxera, 3 acres, of which 2 acres are good for only one crop more; planted to Riparia, 4 acres; Zinfandel grafts succeed best; soil loam; vineyard low lying; all European varieties succumb alike; crop, 29 tons.

Veterans' Home, Yountville.—Total, 35 acres; in bearing, 26 acres; infested by phylloxera, 15 acres, of which 10 acres are good for only one crop more; soil gravelly loam; vineyard upland; exposure east; all European varieties succumb alike; crop 75 tons.
The attacked vines will be uprooted this winter.

John Walker, Yountville.—Total, 26 acres; in bearing, 25 acres; infested by phylloxera, 1 acre; soil loam; vineyard low lying; the Tokay and Zinfandel varieties have proved most resistant; crop, 50 tons.

Jesse Walters, Yountville.—Total, 30 acres; in bearing, 25 acres; infested by phylloxera, 20 acres, of which 3 acres are good for only one crop more; soil loam; vineyard low lying; exposure to wind southwest; all European varieties succumb alike; the attacked vines have received no care; crop, 45 tons.

Mr. Whitton, Yountville.—Total, 10 acres; all in bearing; soil loam; vineyard upland; crop, 14 tons; cooperage, 50,000 gallons, 10,000 of which is oak and 40,000 redwood.

G. Whitton, Yountville.—Total, 20 acres; all in bearing; infested by phylloxera, 5 acres, of which 2 acres are good for only one crop more; soil gravelly; vineyard upland; exposure south and east; crop, 32 tons.

Green Whitton, Yountville.—Total, 16 acres; in bearing, 12 acres; infested by phylloxera, 12 acres, of which 6 acres are good for only one crop more; vineyard upland; exposure east; all European varieties succumb alike; crop, 25 tons.

ST. HELENA DISTRICT.

E. Anguin, Angwin—Total, 6 acres; all in bearing; soil loam; vineyard mountain; exposure west and south; crop, 8 tons.

R. Austin, Angwin.—Total, 30 acres; all in bearing; soil loam; vineyard low lying; exposure north and east; crop, 38 tons.

—— *Blaners, Angwin.*—Total, 5 acres; all in bearing; soil loam; vineyard mountain; crop, 7 tons.

Wm. Geiselman, Angwin.—Total, 90 acres; in bearing, 80 acres; will replant 4 acres; planted to Riparia, 4 acres, of which 3 acres are grafted and not bearing, and 1 acre is not yet grafted; the Cabernet graft has succeeded best; soil loam; vineyard mountain; exposure south and east; crop, 115 tons; cooperage, 90,000 gallons, of which 70,000 is oak and 20,000 is redwood.
On Howell Mountain, known as the Judge Hastings vineyard, there is no phylloxera to speak of, and very few resistants.

E. S. Haas, Angwin.—Total, 25 acres; all in bearing; soil loam; vineyard mountain; crop, 38 tons.

J. W. Hollarhan, Angwin.—Total, 15 acres; all in bearing; soil loam; vineyard mountain; crop, 20 tons.

W. S. Keyes, Angwin.—Total, 100 acres; all in bearing; soil loam; vineyard mountain; exposure south and east; crop, 40 tons.

M. Marseilles, Angwin.—Total, 60 acres; all in bearing; soil loam; vineyard mountain; exposure south; crop, 75 tons.

Murry Bros., Angwin.—Total, 30 acres; all in bearing; soil loam; vineyard mountain; exposure east and south; crop, 40 tons.

O. Norman, Angwin.—Total, 30 acres; all in bearing; soil loam; vineyard mountain; exposure south; crop, 40 tons.

C. Ross, Angwin.—Total, 40 acres; all in bearing; soil loam; vineyard mountain; crop, 50 tons.

N. Samuels, Angwin.—Total, 5 acres; all in bearing; soil loam; vineyard mountain; crop, 8 tons.

S. Turner, Angwin.—Total, 6 acres; all in bearing; soil loam; vineyard mountain; crop, 8 tons.

Peter Tax, Angwin.—Total, 5 acres; all in bearing; soil loam; vineyard mountain; crop, 8 tons.

W. Woodworth, Angwin.—Total, 25 acres; all in bearing; soil loam; vineyard mountain; crop, 38 tons.

T. Workover, Angwin.—Total, 5 acres; all in bearing; soil loam; vineyard mountain; crop, 7 tons.

R. M. Wilson, Angwin.—Total, 25 acres, all in bearing; soil loam; vineyard mountain; exposure south and west; crop, 35 tons.

Wells, Fargo & Co., Angwin.—Total, 45 acres; all in bearing; soil loam; vineyard mountain; exposure east and south; crop, 60 tons; cooperage, 12,000 gallons, of which 4,000 is oak and 8,000 is redwood.

H. Weigland, Angwin.—Total, 20 acres; all in bearing; soil loam; vineyard mountain; crop, 34 tons.

A. Bruck, Bale Station.—Total, 20 acres; all in bearing; infested by phylloxera, 5 acres, of which 1 acre will bear but one crop more; soil loam; vineyard upland; exposure west; crop, 15 tons.

Mrs. L. Coit, Larkmead.—Total, 120 acres; all in bearing; soil loam; vineyard low lying; crop, 150 tons; cooperage, 68,000 gallons, of which 8,000 is oak and 60,000 redwood.
This vineyard was badly frosted in the spring of 1892.

E. J. Barnett, Lidell Post Office, Pope Valley.—Total, 5 acres; all in bearing; soil gravelly loam; vineyard upland; exposure south and east; crop, 6 tons.

C. Hoffman, Lidell Post Office, Pope Valley.—Total, 5 acres; all in bearing; soil gravelly; vineyard low lying; crop, 9 tons.

J. Lawley, Lidell Post Office, Pope Valley.—Total, 10 acres; all in bearing; soil loam; vineyard upland; exposure east; crop, 12 tons.

W. H. Lidell, Lidell Post Office, Pope Valley.—Total, 25 acres; all in bearing; soil loam; vineyard low lying; crop, 23 tons.

B. Ehler, Lodi Station.—Total, 15 acres; all in bearing; soil gravel; vineyard low lying; crop, 40 tons; cooperage, 25,000 gallons, of which 5,000 is oak and 20,000 redwood.
From Lodi north, the phylloxera has attacked very few vineyards.

A. Hirsch, Lodi Station.—Total, 40 acres; all in bearing; infested by phylloxera, 5 acres, of which 1 will bear but one more crop; soil gravelly; vineyard low lying; crop, 40 tons. There is but little phylloxera in this vicinity.

J. Gray, Oakville.—Total, 12 acres; in bearing, 10 acres; infested by phylloxera, 3 acres, of which 1 will bear but one more crop; soil gravelly loam; vineyard low lying; crop, 20 tons.

J. C. Sullinger, Oakville.—Total, 10 acres; all in bearing; infested by phylloxera, 5 acres, 1 of which will bear but one crop more; soil loam; vineyard low lying; crop, 21 tons.

Mrs. C. Wallins, Oakville.—Total, 30 acres; in bearing, 25 acres; infested by phylloxera, 10 acres, 2 of which will bear but one crop more; soil gravelly; vineyard low lying; crop, 38 tons.

C. Ellis, Pope Valley.—Total, 16 acres; all in bearing; soil gravelly loam; vineyard low lying; crop, 20 tons.
The few vineyards in Pope Valley are small, and there are no cellars worthy the name. What vineyards there are will not last long. The frost cut the last crop down a great deal.

A. Mitchell, Pope Valley.—Total, 5 acres; all in bearing; in table grapes, 5 acres; soil gravelly loam; vineyard low lying; crop, 6 tons.

Richard Bros., Pope Valley.—Total, 5 acres; all in bearing; soil loam; vineyard upland; crop, 8 tons.

N. Samuels, Pope Valley.—Total, 10 acres; all in bearing; soil gravelly loam; vineyard upland; crop, 13 tons.

N. Silsbaugh, Pope Valley.—Total, 5 acres; all in bearing; soil loam; vineyard upland; crop, 8 tons.

Stafford & Son, Pope Valley.—Total, 30 acres; all in bearing; soil loam; vineyard upland; crop, 40 tons.

G. Stakemire, Pope Valley.—Total, 6 acres; all in bearing; soil loam; vineyard low lying; crop, 8 tons.

S. Wardner, Pope Valley.—Total, 10 acres; all in bearing; soil loam; vineyard upland; exposure north and west; crop, 14 tons.

J. T. Winchester, Pope Valley.—Total, 8 acres; all in bearing; soil rich loam; vineyard low lying; crop, 15 tons.

W. Woodworth, Pope Valley.—Total, 20 acres; all in bearing; soil loam; vineyard upland; crop, 25 tons.

C. P. Adamson, Rutherford.—Total, 160 acres; all in bearing; planted to Lenoir, 6 acres, all of which are grafted and in bearing; soil gravelly; vineyard low lying; crop, 300 tons; cooperage, 200,000 gallons, of which 50,000 is oak and 150,000 is redwood.
Mr. Adamson likes Lenoir better than Riparia, because it has a faster growth and can be grafted sooner.

J. B. Atkinson, Rutherford.—Total, 110 acres; in bearing, 90 acres; will replant 5 acres; infested by phylloxera, 20 acres; planted to Riparia, 2 acres, all of which are grafted but not bearing; soil loam; vineyard low lying; exposure southwest; no difference in resistance among attacked European vines; crop, 235 tons.
The vineyards in this section are going fast.

W. H. Brockhurst, Rutherford.—Total, 25 acres; in bearing, 23 acres; will replant 3 acres; infested by phylloxera, 5 acres; has only about 200 Riparia roots; soil gravelly loam; vineyard upland; exposure east; crop, 50 tons; cooperage, 25,000 gallons, of which 5,000 is oak and 20,000 redwood.
Mr. Brockhurst is satisfied that Riparia is the best resistant for his soil and location, and will gradually replace his diseased vines.

L. DeBanne, Rutherford.—Total, 5 acres; in bearing, 3 acres; planted to Riparia, 2 acres, which are not yet grafted; soil black gravelly loam; vineyard low lying; Rose of Peru and Tokay have resisted fairly well; vines are taken out as they decay; crop, 7 tons; cooperage, 38,000 gallons, all redwood.

John Dent, Rutherford.—Total, 20 acres; in bearing, 16 acres; infested by phylloxera, 5 acres, of which 2 acres will bear but one crop more; soil gravelly; vineyard low lying; crop, 20 tons.

Mrs. Dinning, Rutherford.—Total, 55 acres; in bearing, 45 acres; infested by phylloxera, 30 acres, of which 20 acres will bear but one crop more; soil gravelly loam; vineyard low lying; no special care given vines attacked; crop, 53 tons.
This vineyard is fast going.

A. Fochetti, Rutherford.—Total, 13 acres; all in bearing; infested by phylloxera, 5 acres, of which 1 acre will bear but one crop more; soil gravelly; vineyard low lying; crop, 30 tons; cooperage, 50,000 gallons, of which 5,000 is oak and 45,000 is redwood.

H. H. Harris, Napa (Vineyard in Rutherford).—Total, 60 acres; in bearing, 41 acres; infested by phylloxera, 20 acres, of which 10 acres is good for but one crop more; planted to Riparia, 19 acres, none of it grafted; soil gravelly; vineyard upland; crop, 138 tons; cooperage, 185,000 gallons, all redwood.
The Riparia is doing finely.

H. W. Helms, Rutherford.—Total, 25 acres; all in bearing; planted to Riparia, 6 acres; none grafted; soil gravelly loam; vineyard upland; exposure east; crop, 40 tons; cooperage, 60,000 gallons, of which 10,000 is oak and 50,000 redwood.

Kinkle Bros., Rutherford.—Total, 20 acres; in bearing, 15 acres; soil reddish loam; vineyard upland; exposure west and south; crop, 30 tons.

J. Lacase, Rutherford.—Total, 10 acres; in bearing, 7 acres; infested by phylloxera, 8 acres, of which 4 acres will bear but one crop more; soil loam; vineyard mountain; exposure south and east; all attacked vines succumb alike; crop, 15 tons.

J. M. Mayfield, Rutherford.—Total, 65 acres; in bearing, 60 acres; infested by phylloxera, 25 acres, of which 5 will bear but one crop more; soil gravelly; vineyard low lying; no difference in attacked vines, as all alike go; no special care given attacked vines; crop, 186 tons; cooperage, 100,000 gallons, of which 25,000 is oak and 75,000 redwood.
This vineyard is gradually dying.

J. J. McIntyre, Rutherford.—Total, 10 acres; all in bearing; soil loam; vineyard low lying; crop, 15 tons.

M. Porter, Rutherford.—Total, 60 acres; in bearing, 40 acres; infested by phylloxera, 30 acres; soil gravelly loam; vineyard low lying; all attacked vines succumb alike; crop, 50 tons.
This vineyard can last but two or three years longer.

Rennie Bros., Rutherford.—Total, 60 acres; in bearing, 55 acres; infested by phylloxera, 20 acres, of which 5 will bear but one crop more; will replant a few acres this winter; planted to Riparia, 3 acres, and to Lenoir, 2 acres; none grafted; soil loam; crop, 80 tons; cooperage, 80,000 gallons, of which 40,000 is oak and 40,000 redwood.

T. L. Rutherford, Rutherford.—Total, 55 acres; in bearing, 53 acres; infested by phylloxera, 2 acres, of which 1 will bear but one crop more; soil gravelly loam; vineyard low lying; all European varieties succumb alike; crop, 110 tons.

Charles Scheggia, Rutherford.—Total, 60 acres; in bearing, 50 acres; infested by phylloxera, 10 acres, of which 5 will bear but one crop more; soil black and gravelly; vineyard upland; exposure southwest; Tokay has resisted fairly well; no special care given attacked vines; crop, 80 tons; cooperage, 70,000 gallons, of which 5,000 is oak and 65,000 redwood.

George Seidberg, Rutherford.—Total, 15 acres; all in bearing; soil loam; vineyard low lying; crop, 25 tons.

Snowball Estate, Rutherford.—Total, 70 acres; in bearing, 60 acres; infested by phylloxera, 20 acres, of which 10 will bear but one crop more; soil thin, light loam; vineyard upland; exposure northeast; no care given attacked vines; crop, 90 tons.
This vineyard is very badly infested.

D. C. Stice, Rutherford.—Total, 5 acres; in bearing, 3 acres; infested by phylloxera, 4 acres, all of which will be pulled up this winter; soil gravelly; vineyard upland; crop, 8 tons.

M. Stice, Rutherford.—Total, 20 acres; all in bearing; infested by phylloxera, 5 acres, of which 2 acres will bear but one crop more; crop, 18 tons.
This vineyard is fast going.

E. J. Van Vleet, Rutherford.—Total, 20 acres; in bearing, 25 acres; in wine grapes, 18 acres; in table grapes, 12 acres; soil loam; vineyard low lying; Tokay has proved fairly resistant; crop, 45 tons.

L. H. Wakefield, Rutherford.—Total, 20 acres; in bearing, 15 acres; infested by phylloxera, 15 acres, all of which will be pulled up this winter; soil gravelly; vineyard low lying; no difference in attacked European vines; no extra pains taken with same; crop, 48 tons.

D. Wood, Rutherford.—Total, 15 acres; in bearing, 10 acres; planted to Riparia, 5 acres, which are not yet grafted; soil loam; vineyard low lying; crop, 16 tons; cooperage, 50,000 gallons, of which 10,000 is oak and 40,000 is redwood.

R. E. Wood, Rutherford.—Total, 40 acres; in bearing, 20 acres; infested by phylloxera, 5 acres, of which 1 acre will bear but one crop more; soil gravelly loam; vineyard upland; exposure west; no special care given attacked vines, which succumb alike; crop, 75 tons.

J. H. Allison, St. Helena.—Total, 15 acres; all in bearing; soil black gravel; vineyard low lying; crop, 20 tons.

T. Amesbury, St. Helena.—Total, 30 acres, all in bearing; infested by phylloxera, 5 acres, of which 1 will bear but one crop more; planted to Lenoir, 3 acres, not grafted; soil stiff loam; vineyard low lying; crop, 20 tons; cooperage, 75,000 gallons, of which 5,000 is oak and 70,000 redwood.

—— Arnold, St. Helena.—Total, 30 acres; in bearing, 25 acres; infested by phylloxera, 20 acres, of which 5 will bear but one crop more; soil gravelly; vineyard low lying. This vineyard is in a very bad condition on account of the phylloxera.

M. G. Bale, St. Helena.—Total, 15 acres; in bearing, 12 acres; infested by phylloxera, 8 acres, of which 3 will bear but one crop more; soil stiff loam; vineyard low lying; crop, 25 tons. This vineyard is rapidly going.

J. R. Beardsley, St. Helena.—Total, 17 acres; all in bearing; soil gravelly; vineyard low lying; crop, 25 tons.

Estate of Dr. H. W. Beers, St. Helena.—Total, 20 acres; all in bearing; infested by phylloxera, 5 acres, of which 2 acres are good for only one crop more; soil gravelly; vineyard upland; crop, 34 tons.

J. L. Benner, St. Helena.—Total, 20 acres; in bearing, 18 acres; planted to Lenoir, 1¼ acres; none grafted; soil black gravelly loam; vineyard low lying; crop, 40 tons.

W. Berk, St. Helena.—Total, 20 acres; all in bearing; infested by phylloxera, 1 acre; soil loam; vineyard low lying; crop, 40 tons.

Beringer Bros., St. Helena.—Total, 135 acres; in bearing, 100 acres; a few acres will be replanted this winter; planted to Riparia, 35 acres, none grafted; soil, on the hill, 100 acres, is deep loam, while in the valley it is stiff adobe; crop, 400 tons; cooperage, 300,000 gallons, of which 120,000 is oak and 180,000 redwood.
The Riparia has been set out on 35 acres of rather cold and stiff land. Half was planted with rooted vines, and in the following year cuttings were set out. The cuttings made a more vigorous growth than the rooted vines, and will be ready to graft at the same time, surprising as this may seem. Mr. Beringer favors the Lenoir for the dry upland, and the Riparia for wet or heavy soil. He advocates setting out the cuttings just as early in the season as possible, the earlier the better. The 35 acres of lowland vineyard will be grafted to approved brandy varieties.

Paul Bieber, St. Helena.—Total, 13 acres; all in bearing; infested by phylloxera, 2 acres; soil black gravel; vineyard low lying; all European varieties succumb alike; crop, 30 tons; cooperage, 50,000 gallons, of which 5,000 is oak and 45,000 redwood.

J. M. L. Black, St. Helena.—Total, 30 acres; all in bearing; infested by phylloxera, 5 acres, of which 2 acres are good for only one crop more; soil gravelly; vineyard low lying; crop, 40 tons.

O. S. Blackman, St. Helena.—Total, 20 acres; all in bearing; infested by phylloxera, 5 acres, of which 2 acres are good for only one crop more; soil gravelly; vineyard low lying; crop, 38 tons.

J. Bottimer, St. Helena.—Total, 20 acres; in bearing, 18 acres; planted to Riparia, 1 acre, and to Lenoir, 1 acre, not grafted; soil gravelly loam; vineyard low lying; crop, 30 tons; cooperage, 5,000 gallons, all redwood.
So far the Riparia has done well, and it is most in favor.

W. B. Bourn, St. Helena.—Total, 420 acres; in bearing, 380 acres; doubtful if any will be replanted; infested by phylloxera, 60 acres, of which 20 will bear but one crop more; planted to Riparia, 1 acre, and to Lenoir, ½ acre, which are grafted but not bearing; the Burgundy grafts are doing well; soil gravel and loam; vineyard low lying and upland; exposure west and south; Zinfandel has proved the poorest resistant among foreign stocks, and Burger the best; vines partially uprooted as attacked; crop, 530 tons; cooperage, 1,500,000 gallons, of which 1,000,000 is oak and 500,000 redwood.

Mrs. Bourn, St. Helena.—Total, 75 acres; in bearing, 70 acres; infested by phylloxera, 10 acres, of which 2 acres will bear but one crop more; soil loam; vineyard low lying; crop, 100 tons.

George Breitenbecher, St. Helena.—Total, 10 acres; all in bearing; infested by phylloxera, 2 acres, of which 1 acre is good for only one crop more; soil loam; vineyard low lying; crop, 18 tons.

Bretti Bros., St. Helena.—Cooperage, 35,000 gallons, of which 17,000 is oak and 18,000 is redwood.

3—N

Carver Estate, St. Helena.—Total, 16 acres; all in bearing; infested by phylloxera, 2 acres, of which 1 acre is good for only one crop more; soil gravelly; vineyard low lying all European varieties succumb alike; crop, 10 tons.
This vineyard is going slowly but surely.

W. H. Castner, St. Helena.—Total, 30 acres; all in bearing; infested by phylloxera, 6 acres, of which 1 acre is good for only one crop more; soil gravelly; vineyard low lying; crop, 70 tons.
Vineyards in this vicinity are badly affected with phylloxera, and comparatively few of the owners have planted resistants.

W. H. Castner, Jr., St. Helena.—Total, 30 acres; all in bearing; infested by phylloxera, 3 acres, of which 1 acre will bear but one crop more; soil loam; vineyard low lying; crop, 50 tons; cooperage, 40,000 gallons, all redwood.

Chabot Estate, St. Helena.—Total, 25 acres; in bearing, 20 acres; will replant 4 or 5 acres; planted to Riparia, 10 acres, of which 4 are grafted but not bearing, and 6 not yet grafted; soil gravelly loam; vineyard low lying and upland; exposure east and southeast; Burger has resisted fairly well; crop, 40 tons; cooperage, 15,000 gallons, of which 3,000 is oak and 12,000 redwood.

A. Chaix, St. Helena.—Total, 25 acres; all in bearing; soil loam; vineyard upland; crop, 63 tons; cooperage, 8,000 gallons, all redwood.

M. Chevalier, St. Helena.—Total, 40 acres; all in bearing; soil loam; vineyard mountain; exposure north; crop, 120 tons; cooperage, 50,000 gallons, of which 10,000 gallons is oak and 40,000 redwood.
Mr. Chevalier has just completed a very fine stone cellar, with a slate roof and of large capacity. He has expended $20,000 or thereabouts in improvements. His vineyard is 4 miles from St. Helena on the Spring Mountain road. No phylloxera has yet appeared in this or the neighboring vineyards—or but little. There are few resistants in this locality.

D. Cole, St. Helena.—Total, 30 acres; in bearing, 28 acres; infested by phylloxera, 3 acres, of which 1 will bear but one crop more; soil gravelly loam; vineyard low lying; crop, 56 tons.

Conrad & Co., St. Helena.—Total, 70 acres; all in bearing; soil loam; vineyard mountain; exposure north and west; crop, 200 tons.
This vineyard is on Spring Mountain, which is a favored locality, as phylloxera has not yet made its appearance, and frost did no damage in the spring of 1892.

M. C. Cook, St. Helena.—Total, 5 acres; all in bearing; soil loam; vineyard low lying; crop, 8 tons.

W. Courtay, St. Helena.—Total, 35 acres; all in bearing; soil reddish loam; vineyard upland; exposure north and west; crop, 82 tons.

T. Cragen, St. Helena.—Total, 20 acres; in bearing, 15 acres; will replant 5 acres; infested by phylloxera, 15 acres, of which 5 will bear but one crop more; soil gravelly loam; vineyard low lying; crop, 30 tons.

Dr. G. B. Crane, St. Helena.—Total, 115 acres; in bearing, 112 acres; infested by phylloxera, 10 acres, 3 of which will bear but one crop more; soil gravelly; vineyard low lying; no difference among attacked European vines; crop, 210 tons.
The soil is rather light in portions of the vineyard, and the gravel is washed from the hills. Portions of the vineyard were rooted up last year. More vines are going fast, and the vineyard can last but a few years longer.

J. Cresley, St. Helena.—Total, 34 acres; in bearing, 32 acres; infested by phylloxera, 5 acres, of which 2 acres are good for only one crop more; crop, 44 tons.
This vineyard was badly frosted.

J. Dowdell, St. Helena.—Total, 20 acres; in bearing, 18 acres; soil gravel and black loam; vineyard low lying; Tokay has proved fairly resistant; crop, 30 tons.
Mr Dowdell has charge of Bourn's cellar, and makes wine there.

W. Eckert, St. Helena.—Total, 28 acres; in bearing, 24 acres; infested by phylloxera, 4 acres, of which 3 acres are good for only one crop more; soil loam; vineyard low lying; all European varieties succumb alike; crop, 55 tons.
Will uproot 3 or 4 acres in the spring.

Edge Hill Vineyard Co., St. Helena.—Total, 150 acres; in bearing, 140 acres; will replant 10 to 15 acres; infested by phylloxera, 25 acres, of which 12 acres are good for only one crop more; planted to Lenoir, 10 acres, which are not yet grafted; soil loam; vineyard upland; all European varieties succumb alike; crop, 210 tons; cooperage, 256,000 gallons, of which 125,000 is oak and 131,000 is redwood.
"In replanting will set out Lenoir on hillside and Riparia in the valley. I think this practice best. In setting out resistants one needs to select soil adapted to the different kinds."

S. Ewer, St. Helena.—Total, 90 acres; in bearing, 85 acres; infested by phylloxera, 10 acres, of which 7 is good for only one crop more; planted to Riparia, 3 acres, to Lenoir, 2 acres, all of which are grafted but not bearing; Burgundy and Zinfandel grafts are doing well; soil loam; vineyard low lying; Zinfandel has proved most resistant; crop, 350 tons; cooperage, 250,000 gallons, all of which is redwood.
Lenoir (resistant) does best in this section.

Alex. Eynard, St. Helena.—Total, 25 acres, all of which is in bearing; infested by phylloxera, 5 acres, of which 1 acre is good for only one crop more; soil loam; vineyard upland; exposure west; crop, 60 tons.

G. C. Fountain, St. Helena.—Total, 40 acres; in bearing, 38 acres; will replant 5 or 6 acres; infested by phylloxera, 5 acres, of which 1 acre is good for only one crop more; soil loam; vineyard low lying; exposure west and south; all European varieties succumb alike; crop, 90 tons.
Will replant resistants in the spring.

Same, St. Helena.—Total, 20 acres, in bearing, 15 acres; infested by phylloxera, 10 acres, of which 2 acres are good for only one crop more; soil gravelly; vineyard low lying; crop, 30 tons.
Two years' time will wipe out many of the vineyards in this vicinity, at least the smaller ones, and fearfully decimate the larger ones.

M. Fountain, St. Helena.—Total, 60 acres; all in bearing; infested by phylloxera, 10 acres, of which 3 acres are good for only one crop more; soil gravelly; crop, 75 tons.

F. Fradet, St. Helena (Spring Mountain).—Total, 10 acres; all in bearing; soil loam; vineyard mountain; crop, 25 tons.

Mrs. Fulton, St. Helena.—Total, 10 acres; in bearing, 8 acres; infested by phylloxera, 4 acres, of which 2 acres are good for only one crop more; soil gravelly; vineyard low lying; all European varieties succumb alike; crop, 15 tons.

Mrs. Furness, St. Helena.—Total, 50 acres; all in bearing; crop, 95 tons; cooperage, 25,000 gallons, of which 5,000 is oak and 20,000 is redwood.

Mrs. Gibson, St. Helena.—Total, 14 acres; all in bearing; infested by phylloxera, 2 acres; of which 1 acre is good for only one crop more; soil loam; vineyard low lying; crop, 20 tons.

W. T. Gillahan, St. Helena.—Total, 15 acres; in bearing, 14 acres; infested by phylloxera, 2 acres, of which 1 acre is good for only one crop more; soil loam; vineyard low lying; crop, 13 tons.

L. Handon, St. Helena.—Total, 15 acres; all in bearing; infested by phylloxera, 4 acres, of which 2 acres are good for only one crop more; soil gravelly loam; Zinfandel has proved most resistant of foreign vines; crop, 27 tons; cooperage, 50,000 gallons, of which 20,000 is oak and 30,000 is redwood.

M. Gluttoon, St. Helena.—Total, 15 acres; all in bearing; will replant 2 acres; soil gravelly; vineyard low lying; crop, 40 tons.

J. M. Graham, St. Helena.—Total, 10 acres; all in bearing; infested by phylloxera, 4 acres; of which 1 acre is good for only one crop more; soil gravelly; vineyard low lying; all European varieties succumb alike; crop, 17 tons.

W. H. Gratton, St. Helena.—Total, 75 acres; in bearing, 70 acres; soil gravelly; vineyard low lying; crop, 145 tons.

J. Greer, St. Helena.—Total, 50 acres; all in bearing; infested by phylloxera, 15 acres, of which 3 or 4 acres are good for only one crop more; soil loam; vineyard low lying; crop, 100 tons.

Thomas Greer Estate, St. Helena.—Total, 15 acres; in bearing, 12 acres; infested by phylloxera, 4 acres; soil gravelly; vineyard low lying; crop, 20 tons.
This vineyard is going fast. Half an acre or more will be taken up in the spring.

C. C. Griffith, St. Helena.—Total, 5 acres; all in bearing; soil gravelly loam; vineyard low lying; exposure west; all European varieties succumb alike; crop, 10 tons.

E. M. Hall, St. Helena.—Total, 100 acres; all in bearing; crop, 170 tons; cooperage, 150,000 gallons, of which 75,000 is oak and 75,000 is redwood.

J. A. Hanna, St. Helena.—Total, 7 acres; all in bearing; infested by phylloxera, 5 acres, of which 3 acres are good for only one crop more; soil gravelly loam; vineyard low lying; exposure southeast; all European varieties succumb alike; crop, 18 acres.

W. Hemes, St. Helena.—Total, 10 acres; in bearing, 8 acres; will replant 1 acre; infested by phylloxera, 5 acres; soil loam and gravel; vineyard low lying; crop, 30 tons.

E. Heyman, St. Helena.—Total, 35 acres; in bearing, 33 acres; infested by phylloxera, 5 acres, of which 1 acre is good for only one crop more; soil gravelly; vineyard low lying; exposure southwest; Tokay has proved most resistant; crop, 55 tons; cooperage, 40,000 gallons, of which 5,000 is oak and 35,000 is redwood.

M. Hudson, St. Helena.—Total, 10 acres; in bearing, 9 acres; infested by phylloxera, 3 acres, of which 1 acre is good for only one crop more; soil gravelly loam; vineyard low lying; exposure southwest; crop, 15 tons.

T. H. Ink, St. Helena.—Total, 120 acres; in bearing, 100 acres; infested by phylloxera, 20 acres, of which 5 acres are good for only one crop more; crop, 200 tons; cooperage, 75,000 gallons, all of which is redwood.

M. F. Inman, St. Helena.—Total, 18 acres; in bearing, 17 acres; infested by phylloxera, 4 acres, of which 2 acres are good for only one crop more; soil black gravel; vineyard low lying; exposure south; all European varieties succumb alike; crop, 30 tons.

A. Jones, St. Helena.—Total, 40 acres; in bearing, 38 acres; infested by phylloxera, 5 acres, of which 1 acre is good for only one crop more; soil loam; vineyard low lying; exposure southeast; crop, 75 tons.

Orrin Jones, St. Helena.—Total, 45 acres; all in bearing; infested by phylloxera, 5 acres, of which 2 acres are good for only one crop more; soil gravelly; vineyard low lying; crop, 100 tons.

M. Kemper, St. Helena.—Total, 50 acres; in bearing, 45 acres; infested by phylloxera, 10 acres, of which 3 acres are good for only one crop more; soil gravelly; vineyard low lying; crop, 65 tons.

F. Kief, St. Helena.—Total, 20 acres; all in bearing; infested by phylloxera, 5 acres, of which 2 acres are good for one year more; soil gravelly loam; vineyard low lying; crop, 38 tons.

M. Kilduff, St. Helena.—Total, 25 acres; all in bearing; soil loam; vineyard upland; exposure east; crop, 52 tons.

A. Klotz, St. Helena.—Total, 10 acres; all in bearing; soil loamy; vineyard low lying; exposure south; crop, 19 tons.

F. Kraft, St. Helena.—Total, 25 acres; all in bearing; will replant 5 acres; planted to Riparia, 2 acres; all grafted and bearing; soil gravelly; vineyard low lying; Chasselas Fontainebleau has proved most resistant of European vines; crop, 40 tons; cooperage, 35,000 gallons, of which 5,000 is oak and 30,000 is redwood.

Krug Estate, St. Helena.—Total, 75 acres; in bearing, 35 acres; will replant 5 or 10 acres; planted to Riparia, 30 acres, and to Lenoir, 5 acres, 15 of which are grafted but not bearing, and 20 are not grafted; the Mondeuse, Cabernet Sauvignon, Burger, Cabernet Franc, and other grafts have succeeded equally well; soil clayey adobe; vineyard low lying; Riesling has proved the most resistant; the attacked vines have received no special treatment; crop, 60 tons; cooperage, 250,000 gallons, of which 75,000 is oak and 175,000 is redwood. On 15 acres or so Mr. Krug, three or four years ago, planted Riparias between rows of European varieties. The latter are now decayed, eaten up by phylloxera, and the resistants are in excellent condition, and will be grafted. Near the river bank on this place Mr. Krug planted Riparia, ten or eleven years ago. They have grown luxuriantly, and innumerable cuttings have been taken from them. Here Riparias are most in favor, such being the estimation in which Mr. Krug held them. The soil is heavy, shading to clay or adobe in places.

Mrs. Laurent, St. Helena.—Total, 50 acres; in bearing, 48 acres; infested by phylloxera, 5 acres, of which 2 acres are good for only one year more; soil stiff loam; vineyard low lying; exposure east and south; all European varieties succumb alike; crop, 75 tons; cooperage, 75,000 gallons, of which 15,000 is oak and 60,000 redwood.

M. Lazarus, St. Helena.—Total, 9 acres; all in bearing; infested by phylloxera, 1 acre; soil gravelly; vineyard low lying; crop, 10 tons.
As in other vineyards near by, the phylloxera is gradually spreading and the outlook is not very cheering.

Mrs. Leathold, St. Helena.—Total, 12 acres; all in bearing; will replant 1 acre; crop, 20 tons.

A. W. Lemme, St. Helena.—Total, 80 acres; all in bearing; soil loamy; vineyard mountain; exposure northwest; crop, 280 tons; cooperage, 75,000 gallons, of which 5,000 is oak and 70,000 is redwood.

H. J. Lewelling, St. Helena.—Total, 175 acres; in bearing, 170 acres; infested by phylloxera, 50 acres, of which 20 acres are good for only one crop more; soil loam; vineyard low lying; Tokay has proved most resistant; crop, 200 tons.
Phylloxera is spreading.

T. E. Lockwood, St. Helena.—Total, 10 acres; all in bearing; infested by phylloxera, 1 acre; soil black gravel; vineyard low lying; all European varieties succumb alike; crop, 16 tons.

F. W. Loeber, St. Helena.—Total, 5 acres; all in bearing; soil loam; vineyard low lying; crop, 12 tons.

W. W. Lyman, St. Helena.—Total, 100 acres; all in bearing; soil gravelly loam; vineyard low lying; all European varieties succumb alike; crop, 180 tons.
This vineyard was badly frosted last spring.

S. H. Mather, St. Helena.—Total, 15 acres; all in bearing; infested by phylloxera, 10 acres, of which 2 acres are good for only one crop more; soil loam; vineyard upland; crop, 60 tons.
Phylloxera will work great havoc in this vineyard in the next year or two.

W. Mathewson, St. Helena.—Total, 15 acres; in bearing, 13 acres; soil loam; vineyard low lying; crop, 15 tons.
Frost cut the yield down one half or one third in many vineyards in this vicinity.

H. Marki, St. Helena.—Total, 12 acres; all in bearing; infested by phylloxera, 5 or 6 acres, of which 4 acres are good for only one crop more; soil gravelly; vineyard low lying; exposure west; Tokay and Zinfandel have proved the most resistant of vinifera; the attacked vines have received little care; crop, 20 tons.

Mrs. McComb, St. Helena.—Total, 15 acres; in bearing, 10 acres; infested by phylloxera, 7 acres, of which 3 acres are good for only one crop more; soil loam and gravel; vineyard low lying; all European varieties succumb alike; the attacked vines have received little care; crop, 25 tons.

McCord Bros., St. Helena.—Total, 40 acres; all in bearing; soil loam; vineyard low lying; all European varieties succumb alike; crop, 140 tons; cooperage, 100,000 gallons, mostly redwood.

C. T. McEachran, St. Helena.—Total, 40 acres; all in bearing; soil gravelly; vineyard low lying; crop, 75 tons; cooperage, 40,000 gallons, of which 10,000 is oak and 30,000 is redwood.

A. McFarland, St. Helena.—Total, 35 acres; all in bearing; infested by phylloxera, 2 acres, of which 1 acre is good for only one crop more; soil loam and gravel; vineyard upland; crop, 60 tons.

J. A. McGuire, St. Helena.—Total, 26 acres; all in bearing; soil loam; vineyard upland; exposure north and west; crop, 70 tons.

George Mee, St Helena.—Total, 35 acres; in bearing, 34 acres; very little is infested by phylloxera; soil fine loam; some of the vineyard is level and some hillside; exposure southwest; all European varieties have succumbed alike; crop, 50 tons.

Meridith Estate, St. Helena.—Total, 10 acres; all in bearing; infested by phylloxera, 4 acres, of which one acre is good for only one crop more; soil gravelly; vineyard low lying; all European varieties succumb alike; crop, 18 tons.

Mrs. Meridith, St. Helena.—Total, 12 acres; all in bearing; infested by phylloxera, 5 acres, of which one acre is good for only one crop more; soil rocky loam; vineyard upland; crop, 20 tons.

Mr. Merk, St. Helena.—Total, 15 acres; all in bearing; soil loam; vineyard mountain; exposure north and west; crop, 50 tons.

Merriam Bros., St. Helena.—Total, 25 acres; in bearing, 23 acres; has some phylloxera; soil black gravel; vineyard low lying; crop, 60 tons; cooperage, 30,000 gallons, of which 10,000 is oak and 20,000 is redwood.
In three or four years no vines will be left.

—— Metcalf, St. Helena.—Total, 10 acres; in bearing, 8 acres; infested by phylloxera, 4 acres, 1 acre of which is good for only one crop more; soil gravelly; vineyard low lying; crop, 10 tons.

J. Miley, St. Helena.—Total, 30 acres; all in bearing; infested by phylloxera, 4 acres, of which 1 acre is good for only one crop more; soil gravelly loam; vineyard low lying; crop, 45 tons; cooperage, 50,000 gallons, of which 5,000 is oak and 45,000 is redwood.

W. Miley, St. Helena.—Total, 16 acres; all in bearing; infested by phylloxera, 4 acres, of which 1 acre is good for only one crop more; soil gravelly; vineyard low lying; crop, 25 tons.

M. Moding, St. Helena.—Total, 30 acres; all in bearing; soil loam; vineyard mountain; exposure west and north; crop, 75 tons.

Mrs. Morel, St. Helena.—Total, 14 acres; in bearing, 12 acres; infested by phylloxera, 5 acres, of which 1 acre is good for only one crop more; soil gravelly loam; vineyard low lying; crop, 12 tons.

C. Mosley, St. Helena.—Total, 10 acres; all in bearing; infested by phylloxera, 3 acres, of which 1 acre is good for only one crop more; soil gravelly; vineyard low lying; crop, 16 tons.

Mrs. Munk, St. Helena.—Total, 10 acres; in bearing, 9 acres; infested by phylloxera, 1 acre; soil loamy; vineyard lowland; exposure south and east; all European varieties succumb alike; crop, 16 tons.

M. Nickerson, St. Helena.—Total, 30 acres; all in bearing; soil gravelly; vineyard low lying; crop, 50 tons.

J. S. Noble, St. Helena.—Total, 15 acres; all in bearing; infested by phylloxera, 15 acres, of which 2 acres are good for only one crop more; soil gravelly; vineyard low lying; crop, 25 tons.

J. Norton, St. Helena.—Total, 30 acres; all in bearing; soil loam; vineyard low lying; crop, 50 tons; cooperage, 40,000 gallons, all of which is redwood.

E. P. Palmer, St. Helena.—Total, 40 acres; all in bearing; has a few Lenoir and Riparia vines not grafted; soil loam; vineyard upland; exposure east and south; crop, 85 tons.

Mr. Palmer has probably more experience with resistants than most any other person in the county. For several years he has made a study of different kinds of resistants, and has read, has experimented, and has traveled for observation. His experience he has embodied in articles in the "Pacific Wine and Spirit Review," and other papers.

"Although I have found no instance," said Mr. P., "in this State where Lenoirs were destroyed on their own roots previous to 1892, I give the preference to Riparia. With others, I served as a committee to visit vineyards in this county, where resistants had been planted. We found, in 1890, no evidence where the Lenoir had been destroyed on its own roots; but in 1892, as one of a committee, found a large number of Lenoirs which had been destroyed on their own roots by phylloxera. Lenoir will not thrive on cold, wet soil, and they easily succumb on such soil to the phylloxera, if the insect commences to work in the vineyard. My faith in Lenoir, once strong, is shaken by past experience, and I give first preference to Riparia. I shall not set out any more Lenoir. It is a strange thing, as Judge Stanly said, that Lenoir has proved resistant in some soils and in others non-resistant. The soil evidently has much to do with resistance of Lenoir. This is very evident. The fact that the Lenoir's habitat is on high, dry lands is probably a reason why it does not succeed on the low lands. The Riparia's habitat is more in the low lands. Certainly in this county it succeeds better than Lenoir. Those who are enthusiastic regarding Lenoir have had but a limited experience. I have found places in this valley where Lenoir succeeded in adobe soil; but in other places, in like soil, it failed. My observation is that Lenoir is unreliable. In one case we found, as cited above, 4,000 Lenoirs killed by phylloxera, on its own roots. I look upon planting Lenoir as an experiment. The man who plants them is taking chances, and one does not care to do that at this day. Lenoir grows faster on upland" (and yet, H. Hagen, of Napa, has admirably succeed with Riparias on his upland). "In six years' time Riparia will make good growth and bring good results. Colonel Fry's foreman says in his (Fry's) vineyard, Lenoir was killed by phylloxera. This is the only place I found where Lenoir had been killed by phylloxera when planted on upland, in dry, gravelly soil. Riparia on this ranch (Colonel Fry's) has proved all that could be desired. I am satisfied one cannot find in this State a case where Riparia has been destroyed by phylloxera when on its own roots; *i. e.*, no graft inserted. The only true way to judge of the two (Lenoir and Riparia) is to base that judgment upon cases where they are planted—growing on their own roots. Riparias are by far the most reliable. This is my conclusion after long years of observation and critical examination."

The following extract is from a report Mr. Palmer made to the St. Helena Viticultural Association in September, 1892: "In the spring of 1882 Mr. Groezinger set out in his vineyard at Yountville, three blocks of cuttings purchased as Lenoirs. This spring we found about 400 vines sick or diseased from phylloxera. The man who grafted them did not consider Lenoir phylloxera proof. These Lenoirs were placed in low, clay soil, having not much depth. Mr. Crabb has set out 20 acres of Lenoir this season on dry ground. We condemn the planting of Lenoir in low, wet (clay) soil. While Riparia would not be in its native element in such soil, yet having shown a better adaptation than Lenoir for cold and wet, heavy land, it stands preëminently in the lead as a resistant."

T. Parrott, St. Helena.—Total, 120 acres; in bearing, 100 acres; infested by phylloxera, 3 acres, of which 1 acre is good for only one crop more; soil rocky loam; vineyard upland; exposure north and east; all European varieties succumb alike; crop, 200 tons; cooperage, 100,000 gallons, of which 60,000 is oak and 40,000 is redwood.

"It may be that many vineyardists have paid little attention to the different attacks of phylloxera on different varieties, but the almost invariable answer is: 'I have failed to note any difference.' Likewise, in case of phylloxera-infected vines, the invariable method has been to treat in no special way except in very rare instances, and then a few vines only have been experimented with."

Olive trees are planted among the vines in a portion of this vineyard.

H. A. Pellet, St. Helena.—Total, 45 acres; all in bearing; will replant 3 acres; infested by phylloxera, 10 acres, of which 3 acres are good for only one crop more; soil gravelly; vineyard low lying; all European varieties succumb alike; crop, 94 tons; cooperage, 60,000 gallons, of which 10,000 is oak and 50,000 is redwood.

Every year some of the vines in this vineyard go by phylloxera, but will replant resistants to take their place. Riparia is favored.

J. Peterson, St. Helena.—Total, 36 acres; all in bearing; infested by phylloxera, 10 acres, of which 3 acres are good for only one crop more; soil gravelly; vineyard low lying; Burger has proved the most resistant; crop, 117 tons.

This vineyard is going fast.

Same, St. Helena.—Total, 34 acres; all in bearing; will replant 2 acres to Riparia; planted to Riparia, 2 acres, grafted but not bearing; Zinfandel has succeeded best on resistants; am satisfied with the resistants.

Peterson Bros., St. Helena.—Total, 34 acres; all in bearing; will replant 2 acres to Riparia; infested by phylloxera, 6 acres; soil loam; vineyard low lying; crop, 50 tons.

A. Pfiester, St. Helena.—Total, 10 acres; in bearing, 8 acres; infested by phylloxera, 3 acres, of which 1 acre is good for one crop more; soil black gravel; vineyard low lying.

W. L. Phillips, St. Helena.—Total, 50 acres; all in bearing; infested by phylloxera, 10 acres, of which 2 acres are good for only one crop more; soil loam; vineyard low lying; crop, 90 tons.

John M. Pike, St. Helena.—Total, 80 acres; in bearing, 75 acres; infested by phylloxera, 20 acres, of which 5 acres are good for only one crop more; soil gravelly loam; vineyard low lying; exposure south; all European varieties succumb alike; crop, 125 tons; cooperage, 75,000 gallons, of which 15,000 is oak and 60,000 is redwood.

Dr. M. B. Pond, St. Helena.—Total, 10 acres; in bearing, 9 acres; infested by phylloxera, 2 acres, of which 1 acre is good for only one crop more; soil gravelly; vineyard low lying; crop, 24 tons.

Mrs. A. J. Pope, St. Helena.—Total, 12 acres; in bearing 8 acres; will replant 4 acres; infested by phylloxera, 10 acres, of which 4 acres are good for only one crop more; soil gravelly; vineyard low lying; all European varieties succumb alike; no care has been taken of the attacked vines; crop, 21 tons.
This vineyard is going very rapidly.

Geo. Pratt, St. Helena.—Total, 37 acres; in bearing, 23 acres; will replant 1 acre; planted to Lenoir, 14 acres; the Sauvignon Vert grafts are most successful; soil gravelly loam; vineyard low lying; all European varieties succumb alike; crop, 45 tons.
Lenoir is very popular here.

R. H. Pratt, St. Helena.—Total, 20 acres; all in bearing; infested by phylloxera, 5 acres, of which 1 acre is good for only one crop more; soil gravelly loam; vineyard upland; exposure west; crop, 37 tons.

—— Pugh, St. Helena.—Total, 20 acres; all in bearing; infested by phylloxera, 5 acres, of which 1 acre is good for only one crop more; crop, 35 tons.

A. Kampendahl, St. Helena.—Total, 20 acres; all in bearing; there is very little infested by phylloxera; crop, 50 tons; cooperage, 60,000 gallons, of which 10,000 is oak and 50,000 is redwood.

—— Rattan, St. Helena.—Total, 30 acres; all in bearing; soil gravelly; vineyard low lying; crop, 45 tons.

M. Ridet, St. Helena.—Total, 9 acres; all in bearing; soil red loam; vineyard upland; exposure northeast; crop, 22 tons.

Mrs. Romero, St. Helena.—Total, 5 acres; all in bearing; soil rocky; vineyard low lying; exposure east; crop, 12 tons.

A. Rossi, St. Helena.—Total, 50 acres; in bearing, 45 acres; infested by phylloxera, 10 acres, 4 of which will bear but one crop more; soil gravelly; vineyard low lying; no difference among attacked European vines; crop, 65 tons.

M. Roulet, St. Helena.—Total, 9½ acres; in bearing, 9 acres; infested by phylloxera, 2 acres, half of which will bear but one crop more; soil black loam; vineyard low lying; crop, 15 tons; cooperage, 20,000 gallons, of which 5,000 is oak and 15,000 redwood.

L. Sander, St. Helena.—Total, 50 acres; in bearing, 40 acres; will replant 5 acres to Riparia; infested by phylloxera, 25 acres, 10 of which will bear but one crop more; soil loam; vineyard low lying; no difference among attacked European varieties; crop, 75 tons; cooperage, 40,000 gallons, all redwood.

M. Sawyer, St. Helena.—Total, 30 acres; all in bearing; infested by phylloxera, 5 acres, 2 of which will have but one crop more; soil gravelly; vineyard low lying; crop, 50 tons.

Geo. Schönwald, St. Helena.—Total, 34 acres; in bearing, 30 acres; infested by phylloxera, 15 acres, 4 of which will bear but one crop more; planted to Riparia, 10 acres, all grafted and bearing; Cabernet Sauvignon, Carignan, etc., have done well on Riparia; soil gravelly; vineyard low lying; crop, 80 tons; cooperage, 50,000 gallons, of which 40,000 is oak and 10,000 redwood.
Mr. Schönwald finds that the Riparia is a most satisfactory stock. He has experimented with Clinton, but it is not resistant. He is not certain about the Californica.

Jacob Schram, St. Helena.—Total, 100 acres; all in bearing; soil loam; vineyard mountain; exposure south and east; crop, 360 tons; cooperage, 100,000 gallons, of which 25,000 is oak and 75,000 is redwood.
This vineyard, unlike many in the St. Helena District, was not touched by frost in the spring of 1892. It bore a good crop, consequently. The vineyard is on the summit of the range of hills north and west of St. Helena. "I am always lucky about my crop," said Mr. Schram.

Frank Sciaroni, St. Helena.—Cooperage, 100,000 gallons, of which 25,000 is oak and 75,000 redwood.

L. Lindner, St. Helena.—Total, 15 acres; all in bearing; infested by phylloxera, 3 acres, of which 1 acre is good for only one crop more; soil loam; vineyard low lying; crop, 19 tons.

Mrs. Sheehan, St. Helena.—Total, 22 acres; all in bearing; soil loam; vineyard upland; exposure east and south; crop, 58 tons.
This vineyard is on Spring Mountain, and has no phylloxera.

W. R. Sheehan, St. Helena.—Total, 12 acres; in bearing, 7 acres; soil loam; vineyard upland; exposure east; crop, 19 tons.
This vineyard is on Spring Mountain.

M. Shepherdson, St. Helena.—Total, 10 acres; in bearing, 9 acres; soil gravelly loam; vineyard upland; exposure west; crop, 22 tons.

Harry Simmonds, St. Helena.—Total, 12 acres; all in bearing; infested by phylloxera, 2 acres, of which 1 acre is good for only one crop more; soil gravelly; vineyard low lying; crop, 14 tons.

F. Soto, St. Helena.—Total, 14 acres; all in bearing; soil deep reddish loam; vineyard mountain; exposure east; crop, 48 tons.

E. Spear, St. Helena.—Total, 5 acres; all in bearing; infested by phylloxera, 1 acre; soil gravelly loam; vineyard low lying; no special care given attacked vines; crop, 9 tons.

R. L. Spurr, St. Helena.—Total, 27 acres; in bearing, 24 acres; infested by phylloxera, 15 acres, 5 of which will bear but one crop more; soil gravelly loam; vineyard low lying; no difference in attacked vines; crop, 65 tons.
This vineyard is going fast, and will last but two or three years. Grain and fruit will replace the vineyards in this locality shortly.

Henry Stairs, St. Helena.—Total, 12 acres; all in bearing; soil loam; vineyard mountain; crop, 32 tons.

A. Stamer, St. Helena.—Total, 6 acres; all in bearing; soil gravelly; vineyard low lying; crop, 10 tons; cooperage, 100,000 gallons, of which 10,000 is oak and 90,000 redwood.

Same, St. Helena.—Total, 5 acres; all in bearing; soil loam; vineyard mountain; exposure east; crop, 14 tons.

Starr Estate, St. Helena.—Total, 36 acres; all in bearing; infested by phylloxera, 6 acres, of which 2 will bear but one more crop; soil loam; vineyard low lying; crop, 50 tons.

Mrs. Tainter, St. Helena.—Total, 10 acres; all in bearing; infested by phylloxera, 2 acres, of which 1 acre is good for only one year more; soil gravelly; vineyard low lying; crop, 16 tons.

W. Templar, St. Helena.—Total, 7 acres; planted to Lenoir, 2 acres, which are not yet grafted; soil gravelly loam; vineyard low lying; crop, 60 tons.

C. Tiederman, St. Helena.—Total, 15 acres; all in bearing; infested by phylloxera, 2 acres, of which 1 acre is good for only one year more; soil gravelly; vineyard low lying; crop, 20 tons.

John Thomann, St. Helena.—Total, 40 acres; all in bearing; soil loam; vineyard mountain; cooperage, 250,000 gallons, half oak and half redwood.
This vineyard is on Howell Mountain and is 6 or 7 years old. No phylloxera has appeared, but many of the vines have dry rot. This is thought to be caused by impoverished soil, as the vines—many of them—were planted where trees were taken out. The same complaint is occasionally made with the valley vineyards. Fungus forms on the stocks and they soon rot and can be kicked over.

Mrs. Tychson, St. Helena.—Total, 60 acres; all in bearing; infested by phylloxera, 10 acres, of which 3 acres are good for only one crop more; soil gravelly; vineyard upland; crop, 75 tons.

M. Van Doren, St. Helena.—Total, 15 acres; all in bearing; soil gravelly; vineyard low lying; crop, 20 tons.

M. Vann, St. Helena.—Total, 30 acres; all in bearing; infested by phylloxera, 5 acres, 1 of which will bear but one crop more; crop, 60 tons; cooperage, 40,000 gallons, all redwood.

Fred. Waille, St. Helena.—Total, 22 acres; in bearing, 15 acres; planted to Riparia, 4 acres, 2 of which are grafted and in bearing, and 2 grafted but not bearing; Mataro has succeeded well on Riparia; soil loam; vineyard low lying; crop, 23 tons.

Thos. Watt, St. Helena.—Total, 20 acres; all in bearing; infested by phylloxera, 5 acres, of which 2 acres are good for only one crop more; soil gravelly; vineyard low lying; crop, 32 tons.

Mrs. H. E. Weinberger, St. Helena.—Total, 50 acres; in bearing, 45 acres; infested by phylloxera, 10 acres, 2 of which will bear but one crop more; soil gravelly loam; vineyard low lying; no special care given attacked vines; crop, 88 tons; cooperage, 75,000 gallons, of which 25,000 is oak and 50,000 redwood.

John H. Wheeler, St. Helena.—Total, 100 acres; in bearing, 90 acres; will plant 20 acres; infested by phylloxera, 50 acres, 10 of which will bear but one crop more; planted to resistants, 25 acres, 15 of which are to Riparia and 10 to Lenoir; of the 25 acres, 15 are grafted and bearing, and 10 grafted but not bearing; soil loam; vineyard low lying; Orleans, Riesling, and Tokay have resisted longest among European varieties; crop, 208 tons; cooperage, 330,000 gallons, 170,000 of which is oak and 160,000 is redwood.

Mr. Wheeler was formerly connected with the State Viticultural Commission, as Chief Executive Officer and as Secretary, and has embodied his experiences and observations in many articles. He finds that the light-bearing vines are the most resistant, and favors Riparia for stock.

H. White, St. Helena.—Total, 15 acres; all in bearing; soil loam; vineyard low lying; crop, 25 tons.

J. W. Williams, St. Helena.—Total, 42 acres; all in bearing; infested by phylloxera, 15 acres, 3 of which will bear but one crop more; soil gravelly; vineyard low lying; crop, 95 tons.

F. Worst, St. Helena.—Total, 25 acres; in bearing, 22 acres; infested by phylloxera, 5 acres, 1 of which will bear but one crop more; soil gravelly loam; vineyard upland; exposure west; crop, 40 tons.

This vineyard is going rapidly.

Worrell & Ward, St. Helena.—Total, 28 acres; in bearing, 24 acres; infested by phylloxera, 15 acres, 5 of which will bear but one crop more; planted to Lenoir, 7 acres; none yet grafted; soil gravelly; vineyard low lying; no particular care given attacked vines, and all go alike; crop, 30 tons; cooperage, 50,000 gallons, all redwood.

The proprietors will pull up 8 acres of vines this winter.

J. York, St. Helena.—Total, 40 acres; in bearing, 35 acres; infested by phylloxera, 20 acres, half of which will bear but one crop more; soil gravelly loam; vineyard low lying; Tokay has been fairly resistant; crop, 100 tons.

W. E. York, St. Helena.—Total, 33 acres; in bearing, 20 acres; infested by phylloxera, 20 acres, of which 5 will bear but one crop more; soil gravelly; vineyard low lying; crop, 64 tons.

Mr. York was one of a committee to inspect the vineyards in the valley last season. He is very much in favor of Riparia, as, generally speaking, Lenoir has not given as great a degree of satisfaction.

E. Zange, St. Helena.—Total, 33 acres; in bearing, 30 acres; planted to Lenoir, 5 acres, 2 of which are not yet grafted; soil gravelly; vineyard low lying; no difference in attacked vines in the valley; crop, 71 tons; cooperage, 60,000 gallons, half oak and half redwood.

Mr. Zange was one of the committee that examined the vineyards where resistants have been planted for several years. He is in favor of Lenoir because of its rapid growth, it being ready to graft much earlier than Riparia.

L. Zierngibl, St. Helena.—Total, 50 acres; all in bearing; soil gravelly; vineyard low lying; crop, 74 tons.

CHILES AND CONN VALLEYS.

Robt. Black, Chiles Valley.—Total, 10 acres; all in bearing; soil loam; vineyard low lying; crop, 14 tons.

J. Booth, Chiles Valley.—Total, 6 acres; all in bearing; soil loam; vineyard low lying; crop, 8 tons.

J. Brown, Chiles Valley.—Total, 25 acres; all in bearing; soil loam; vineyard low lying; crop, 32 tons.

J. B. Chiles, Chiles Valley.—Total, 12 acres; all in bearing; soil loam; vineyard low lying; crop, 16 tons.

"In Chiles Valley proper there are several small vineyards, and in only three or four of these have resistants been planted. The yield this year was very light, on account of the frost in the spring. Phylloxera is attacking the vines, and in a few years there will be but very few vineyards. The valley is small, only 8 or 10 miles long, one quarter to one half of a mile wide, and is 13 miles from St. Helena. It has only one or two cellars."

J. G. Clark, Chiles Valley.—Total, 12 acres; all in bearing; soil loam; vineyard low lying; crop, 16 tons.

Geo. Hussmann, Chiles Valley.—Total, 35 acres; in bearing, 23 acres; planted to Riparia. 3 acres, grafted and bearing, and Æstivalis, 9 acres, which are not yet grafted; the Green Hungarian grafts have succeeded best; soil loam; vineyard low lying; exposure south and west; crop, 65 tons; cooperage, 60,000 gallons, of which 35,000 is oak and 25,000 is redwood.

"I think Riparia the best resistant to use, for it is more easily propagated, and takes scion quicker and better than Lenoir. On Riparia I got 90 per cent grafts by careful work. I see no difference between the black and gray Riparia. My grafts are growing finely and bearing well." This vineyard looks very fine, the soil is rich and deep, and the grafts are growing vigorously. Phylloxera is gaining a foothold in neighboring vineyards. Cuttings are preferred in planting rather than rooted vines, for Mr. Hussmann thinks replanting checks the growth of rooted vines.

Louis Kielman, Chiles Valley.—Total, 11 acres; all in bearing; will replant very little; soil loam; vineyard low lying; crop, 15 tons.

Miss Manning, Chiles Valley.—Total, 10 acres; all in bearing; soil loam; vineyard low lying; crop, 12 tons.

M. Murry, Chiles Valley.—Total, 10 acres; all in bearing; soil loam; vineyard low lying; crop, 12 tons.

R. Rutherford, Chiles Valley.—Total, 12 acres; all in bearing; soil loam; vineyard low lying; crop, 15 tons.

F. Sievers, Chiles Valley.—Total, 25 acres; in bearing, 8 acres; planted to Riparia, 24½ acres, and to Lenoir, 1½ acres; of which 8 acres are grafted and in bearing, 8 acres are grafted and not bearing, and 9 acres are not yet grafted; Sauvignon Vert grafts have proved most successful; soil loam; vineyard upland; exposure west and south; crop, 15 tons; cooperage, 3,000 gallons, of which 2,500 is oak and 500 is redwood.

Mr. Sievers planted resistants wholly, commencing about 6 years ago. From some of his oldest grafts he obtained 35 pounds each year. Sauvignon Vert vines are growing well, and he is well pleased with the success he has had with the resistants. He has mostly Riparia roots, but finds there is a great deal of work in suckering them, and has found resistants must not be grafted too early. If Lenoir and Riparia were equally resistant there is less work with Lenoir, as it grows faster and does not sucker much, if any. Seedling Riparias are not worth bothering with. They grow slowly, the stock is very crooked, and it is almost impossible to graft them well. Rooted cuttings are the best to plant, although replanting them checks their growth, but if propagated (rooted) in the nursery but a small amount of ground is required to grow them, and little area to go over in so doing. If set out in the vineyard before being rooted there is a large amount of ground to go over, and it is far more expensive than if rooted in the nursery. Mr. Sievers sells many cuttings and rooted vines of resistants.

Mrs. R. M. Wheeler, Chiles Valley.—Total, 25 acres; all in bearing; very little is infested by phylloxera; soil loamy; vineyard low lying; crop, 62 tons.

A. B. Alsip, Conn Valley.—Total, 75 acres; in bearing, 73½ acres; planted to Lenoir, 1½ acres, which are not yet grafted; soil gravelly; vineyard upland; exposure west and south; crop, 100 tons; cooperage, 50,000 gallons, of which 20,000 is oak and 30,000 is redwood.

P. Conn, Conn Valley.—Total, 50 acres; in bearing, 45 acres; will replant 5 acres; infested by phylloxera, 10 acres, of which 4 acres are good for only one crop more; soil loam; vineyard upland; exposure south and west; crop, 60 tons.

L. Corthay, Conn Valley.—Total, 35 acres; all in bearing; soil loam; vineyard upland; exposure west and south; crop, 40 tons; cooperage, 35,000 gallons, of which 20,000 is oak and 15,000 is redwood.
The frost cut down the grape crop very badly throughout Conn Valley last spring.

R. Eubanks, Conn Valley.—Total, 27 acres; in bearing, 25 acres; infested by phylloxera, 3 acres, of which 1 acre is good for only one crop more; soil loam; vineyard upland; exposure west and north; all European varieties succumb alike; crop, 20 tons.

Franco-Swiss Co., Conn Valley.—Total, 140 acres; all in bearing; infested by phylloxera, 10 acres, of which 4 acres are good for only one crop more; soil loam; vineyard upland; exposure south and west; crop, 160 tons; cooperage, 150,000 gallons, of which 50,000 is oak and 100,000 is redwood.

L. M. Gianque, Conn Valley.—Total, 20 acres; all in bearing; soil loamy; vineyard upland; exposure west and south; crop, 8 tons.
No phylloxera is acknowledged, but there is some in the neighboring vineyards. Two or three years will see these Conn Valley vineyards very much reduced. The soil is poor and thin, and with diseased vines the outlook is anything but encouraging.

L. Glandon, Conn Valley.—Total, 27 acres; in bearing, 25 acres; infested by phylloxera, 5 acres, of which 2 acres are good for only one crop more; soil loam; vineyard upland; exposure north and west; crop, 30 tons.

A. Gussot, Conn Valley.—Total, 15 acres; all in bearing; soil loam; vineyard upland; crop, 17 tons.

H. Manske, Conn Valley.—Total, 10 acres; all in bearing; soil loam; vineyard upland; crop, 12 tons.

James Matthewson, Conn Valley.—Total, 15 acres; all in bearing; soil loam; vineyard upland; crop, 17 tons.

E. Musgrove, Conn Valley.—Total, 30 acres; all in bearing; soil loam; vineyard upland; exposure west and south; crop 40 tons.

M. Payne, Conn Valley.—Total, 20 acres; all in bearing; soil loam; vineyard upland; crop, 25 tons.

H. Reiman, Conn Valley.—Total, 25 acres; all in bearing; infested by phylloxera, 5 acres; Chasselas Fontainebleau has proved most resistant of European vines; crop, 25 tons; cooperage, 21,000 gallons, all of which is redwood.
This vineyard is situated in the center of Conn Valley. Phylloxera is getting in its deadly work here, and in a few years the vines will all be gone.

Tubbs & Hall, Conn Valley.—Total, 90 acres; all in bearing; will replant 4 acres; soil loam; vineyard upland, exposure west and south; crop, 214 tons; cooperage, 60,000 gallons, of which 30,000 is oak and 30,000 is redwood.
There is no phylloxera acknowledged in the upper end of Conn Valley, but there is a great deal in the lower or south end.

E. Walters, Conn Valley.—Total, 30 acres; in bearing, 25 acres; will replant 4 acres; infested by phylloxera, 10 acres, of which 4 acres are good for only one crop more; crop, 35 tons.

Weston Bros., Conn Valley.—Total 12 acres; in bearing, 10 acres; infested by phylloxera, 3 acres, of which 1 acre is good for only one crop more; soil gravelly; vineyard upland; exposure west and south; Chasselas Fontainebleau has proved most resistant of European vines; crop, 6 tons.
This vineyard is going fast.

CALISTOGA DISTRICT.

F. Ashton, Calistoga.—Total, 20 acres; all in bearing; soil gravelly; vineyard low lying; crop, 30 tons; cooperage, 10,000 gallons, all of which is redwood.

E. Baisley, Calistoga.—Total, 10 acres; all in bearing; soil loam; crop, 17 tons.

B. Beasley, Calistoga.—Total, 10 acres; soil loam; vineyard low lying; crop, 8 tons.

Mrs. Beaumont, Calistoga.—Total, 25 acres; all in bearing; soil loam; vineyard low lying; crop, 40 tons.

Bennet Bros., Calistoga.—Total, 20 acres; all in bearing; soil loam; vineyard low lying; crop, 28 tons.

J. S. Bennet, Calistoga.—Total, 8 acres; all in bearing; soil gravelly loam; crop, 14 tons.

R. Bennet, Calistoga.—Total, 15 acres; all in bearing; soil loam; vineyard low lying; crop, 40 tons.

Bingham Bros., Calistoga.—Total, 30 acres; all in bearing; soil loam; vineyard low lying; crop. 45 tons.

E. L. Bingham, Calistoga.—Total, 12 acres; all in bearing; soil sandy loam; vineyard low lying; crop, 14 tons.

R. Bleole, Calistoga.—Total, 10 acres; all in bearing; soil gravelly; vineyard low lying; crop, 18 tons.

Mrs. P. D. Boomsall, Calistoga.—Total, 36 acres; all in bearing; soil loam; vineyard low lying; crop, 40 tons.

Same, Calistoga.—Total, 35 acres; all in bearing; soil gravelly; vineyard low lying; crop, 50 tons.

J. Borchett, Calistoga.—Total, 20 acres; all in bearing; soil gravelly loam; vineyard low lying; crop, 37 tons.

M. L. Borchett, Calistoga.—Total, 40 acres; all in bearing; soil loam; vineyard low lying; crop, 60 tons.

E. Brown, Calistoga.—Total, 18 acres; all in bearing; soil loam; vineyard low lying; crop, 29 tons.

Same, Calistoga.—Total, 12 acres; all in bearing; soil gravelly; vineyard low lying; crop, 19 tons.

C. M. Burges, Calistoga.—Total, 35 acres; in bearing, 30 acres; infested by phylloxera, 2 acres, of which 1 acre will be good for only one crop more; soil gravelly; vineyard low lying; crop, 40 tons.
This vineyard is not far from Lodi, and is three miles south of Calistoga. Above this point little or no phylloxera has been found in lowland vineyards or on hillside. The season of 1892 was a very poor one, however, because of several frosts in the spring, and a cool summer. The crop is only one third the usual yield.

Mrs. Butler, Calistoga.—Total, 10 acres; all in bearing; soil loam; vineyard low lying; crop, 17 tons.

Same, Calistoga.—Total, 8 acres; all in bearing; soil loam; vineyard low lying; crop, 12 tons.

M. M. Campbell, Calistoga—Total, 10 acres; all in bearing; soil loam; vineyard low lying; crop, 12 tons.

Carver Estate, St. Helena.—Total, 52 acres; in bearing, 50 acres; soil gravelly loam; vineyard low lying; crop, 100 tons.

W. Cole. Calistoga.—Total, 20 acres; all in bearing; soil loam; vineyard low lying; crop, 33 tons.

Same, Calistoga.—Total, 14 acres; all in bearing; soil loam; vineyard low lying; crop, 25 tons.

G. J. Connor, Calistoga.—Total, 6 acres; all in bearing; soil loam and gravel; vineyard low lying; crop, 12 tons.

M. Corlette, Calistoga.—Total, 40 acres; all in bearing; soil gravelly; vineyard low lying; crop, 45 tons.

F. A. Crouch, Calistoga.—Total, 18 acres; all in bearing; soil loam; vineyard upland; crop, 30 tons.

J. V. Culver, Calistoga.—Total, 10 acres; all in bearing; soil loam; vineyard upland; crop, 17 tons.

II. S. Dexter, Calistoga.—Total, 38 acres; in bearing, 35 acres; soil loam; vineyard upland; exposure south and east; crop, 70 tons.
This vineyard is near the Sonoma County line. There is no phylloxera here, and the vines are doing well.

II. Dormay, Calistoga.—Total, 35 acres; all in bearing; soil loam; vineyard upland; crop, 60 tons.

C. Doughty, Calistoga.—Total, 5 acres; all in bearing; soil gravelly; vineyard low lying; crop, 8 tons.

G. Dougherty, Calistoga.—Total, 20 acres; all in bearing; soil loam; vineyard upland; exposure east and north; crop, 30 tons.

W. Eberling, Calistoga.—Total, 8 acres; all in bearing; soil gravelly; vineyard low lying; crop, 14 tons.

Farron & Clydesdale, Calistoga.—Total, 12 acres; soil gravelly; vineyard low lying; crop, 19 tons.

Mrs. S. C. Furness, Calistoga.—Total, 40 acres; all in bearing; soil gravelly; vineyard low lying; crop, 55 tons.

A. G. Garnett, Calistoga.—Total, 50 acres; all in bearing; soil loam; vineyard upland; crop, 70 tons.

John Garnett, Calistoga.—Total, 25 acres; all in bearing; soil loam; vineyard low lying; crop, 45 tons.

J. K. Garnett, Calistoga.—Total, 30 acres; all in bearing; soil gravelly; vineyard low lying; crop, 50 tons; cooperage, 40,000 gallons, all of which is redwood.

A. Grimm & Co., Calistoga.—Total, 60 acres; all in bearing; soil loam; vineyard upland; crop, 180 tons; cooperage, 100,000 gallons, of which 85,000 is oak and 15,000 is redwood.
This vineyard has no phylloxera or resistants, and is doing finely.

Mrs. M. Haley, Calistoga.—Total, 8 acres; all in bearing; soil loam; vineyard upland; crop, 14 tons.

I. M. Hansen, Calistoga.—Total, 10 acres; all in bearing; soil gravelly; vineyard upland; crop, 15 tons.

W. Hansen, Calistoga.—Total, 5 acres; all in bearing; soil loam; vineyard upland; crop, 7 tons.

J. Hintze, Calistoga.—Total, 25 acres; all in bearing; soil gravelly; vineyard upland; crop, 35 tons.

A. Hittle, Calistoga.—Total, 12 acres; all in bearing; soil loam; vineyard upland; crop, 20 tons; cooperage, 30,000 gallons, of which 5,000 is oak and 25,000 is redwood.

A. Hoover, Calistoga.—Total, 10 acres; all in bearing; soil gravelly loam; vineyard low lying; crop, 16 tons.

P. Hopkins, Calistoga.—Total, 17 acres; all in bearing; will plant 10 acres; soil gravelly; vineyard low lying; crop, 30 tons.

S. Kellett, Calistoga.—Total, 60 acres; in bearing, 58 acres; soil soft loam; vineyard low lying; exposure east and south; crop, 8 tons.
Vineyards in this section of the county were fearfully injured by the frost last spring, and at one time the vines were black.

George Lang, Calistoga.—Total, 38 acres; all in bearing; soil gravelly loam; vineyard low lying; crop, 50 tons.

J. Lang, Calistoga.—Total, 18 acres; all in bearing; soil gravelly; vineyard low lying; crop, 24 tons.
There is nothing to note of vineyards in this vicinity, except that they are free from phylloxera, and that they bore only one third of the usual crop this season on account of the frost.

E. Light, Calistoga.—Total, 33 acres; all in bearing; soil gravelly; vineyard upland; crop, 50 tons; cooperage, 60,000 gallons, all of which is redwood.

C. H. Lillie, Calistoga.—Total, 10 acres; all in bearing; soil loam; vineyard low lying; crop, 17 tons.

Mrs. Lloyd, Calistoga.—Total, 32 acres; all in bearing; soil gravelly loam; vineyard low lying; crop, 50 tons.

Davis Manuel, Calistoga.—Total, 50 acres; all in bearing; soil loam; vineyard low lying; crop, 45 tons.

H. Martin, Calistoga.—Total, 10 acres; all in bearing; soil gravelly; vineyard low lying; crop, 22 tons.
This vineyard was badly frosted.

—— *McFee, Calistoga.*—Total, 20 acres; all in bearing; soil loam; vineyard low lying; crop, 30 tons.

J. McGregor, Calistoga.—Total, 8 acres; all in bearing; soil gravelly; vineyard low lying; crop, 15 tons.

C. W. McMerrick, Calistoga.—Total, 15 acres; all in bearing; soil loam; vineyard low lying; crop, 18 tons.

A. Moore, Calistoga.—Total, 5 acres; all in bearing; soil loam and gravelly; crop, 9 tons.

C. J. B. Moore, Calistoga.—Total, 6 acres; all in bearing; soil gravelly; vineyard upland; crop, 10 tons.

W. Phillips, Calistoga.—Total, 40 acres; all in bearing; soil loam and gravelly; vineyard low lying; crop, 100 tons.

W. L. Phillips, Calistoga.—Total, 35 acres; all in bearing; soil loam; vineyard upland; crop, 50 tons.

C. N. Pickett, Calistoga.—Total, 25 acres; all in bearing; soil gravelly; vineyard upland; crop, 40 tons; cooperage, 40,000 gallons, of which 8,000 is oak and 32,000 is redwood.

Same, Calistoga.—Total, 25 acres; all in bearing; soil loam and gravelly; vineyard low lying; crop, 30 tons.

J. G. Randall, Calistoga.—Total, 10 acres; all in bearing; soil loam and gravelly; vineyard low lying; crop, 18 tons.

J. Roberts, Calistoga.—Total, 10 acres; all in bearing; soil gravelly; vineyard upland; crop, 14 tons.
The frost cut down the crop in this section from one half to two thirds.

J. Rutherford, Calistoga.—Total, 20 acres; all in bearing; soil loam; vineyard low lying; crop, 35 tons.

Mrs. Schamp, Calistoga.—Total, 10 acres; all in bearing; soil loam; vineyard low lying; crop, 15 tons.

P. R. Schmidt, Calistoga.—Total, 65 acres; in bearing, 60 acres; will replant several acres; planted to Riparia, 20 acres, and to Lenoir, 10 acres; Sauvignon Vert, Gutedel, Alicante Bouschet, and Semillon grafts have all proved very successful; soil deep reddish loam; vineyard mountain; exposure north and west; crop, 200 tons; cooperage, 45,000 gallons, of which 5,000 is oak and 40,000 is redwood.
"Grafts on resistants have borne two or three good crops. I am very well pleased with results so far. Though the phylloxera has not appeared, am guarding against it. The soil on these hills is deep and rich, and the vines make vigorous growth. Riparia is given the preference as a resistant, though I see no great difference between it and Lenoir. The former is of slower growth, finer grain, and closer texture. The vineyard is looking well, and there has been no frost to speak of here; lemons, oranges, and bananas are growing unprotected. I think my idea of planting resistants at first is an excellent one, for I feel quite secure."

J. Schintzer, Calistoga.—Total, 40 acres; all in bearing; soil gravelly; vineyard upland; crop, 55 tons.

A. Simmons, Calistoga.—Total, 8 acres; all in bearing; soil loam; vineyard low lying; crop, 10 tons.

Mrs. J. H. Smith, Calistoga.—Total, 15 acres; all in bearing; soil loam; vineyard low lying; crop, 22 tons.

R. P. Smith, Calistoga.—Total, 20 acres; all in bearing; soil gravelly; vineyard low lying; crop, 18 tons.
Vineyards in this district, on low lands, were very badly frosted last spring. There is no phylloxera here.

H. Snyder, Calistoga.—Total, 15 acres; all in bearing; soil loam; vineyard upland; crop, 40 tons.
This vineyard is planted on the upland northwest of Calistoga. There are no resistants and no phylloxera in the neighborhood.

T. A. Snyder, Calistoga.—Total, 12 acres; all in bearing; soil shading to adobe; vineyard low lying; crop, 18 tons.

W. Spiers, Calistoga.—Total, 15 acres; all in bearing; soil loam; vineyard upland; crop, 25 tons.

Mrs. Steel, Calistoga.—Total, 15 acres; all in bearing; soil loam; vineyard low lying; crop, 28 tons.

M. Swinacre, Calistoga.—Total, 18 acres; all in bearing; soil loam; vineyard upland; crop, 15 tons.

J. A. Teale, Calistoga.—Total, 10 acres; all in bearing; soil gravelly; vineyard low lying; crop, 14 tons.

P. Teale, Calistoga.—Total, 5 acres; all in bearing; soil loamy and gravelly; vineyard low lying; crop, 7 tons.

A. L. Tubbs, Calistoga.—Total, 220 acres; in bearing, 110 acres; will plant 25 or 30 acres; planted to Riparia, 75 acres, of which 45 are grafted and in bearing, and 30 are not yet grafted; the grafts Cabernet Franc. Merlot, and Malbec have succeeded best, and Chasselas and Sauvignon Blanc do fairly well, but not as well as the above grafts; soil loam; vineyard low lying and upland; crop, 225 tons; cooperage, 350,000 gallons, of which 190,000 is oak and 160,000 is redwood.

"Resistants in this vineyard have been planted for several years, and have proved a success. Preference has been given to Riparia, and the results have been perfectly satisfactory. Will plant more in the spring. I feel confident that Riparia will do well in this section, but do not think much of Lenoir, although Lenoir will do well in localities where Riparia may fail, and *vice versa.* There is no phylloxera in this vicinity yet, and no signs of its coming, yet many vineyardists think it may attack vineyards any season."

G. W. Tucker, Calistoga.—Total, 10 acres; all in bearing; soil loam; vineyard low lying; crop, 18 tons.

J. Tucker, Calistoga.—Total, 10 acres; all in bearing; soil loam; crop, 18 tons.

Thos. Veal, Calistoga.—Total, 7 acres; all in bearing; soil gravelly; vineyard low lying; crop, 12 tons.

Thos. Walsh, Calistoga.—Total, 30 acres; all in bearing; soil sandy loam; vineyard low lying; crop, 60 tons; cooperage, 30,000 gallons, of which 10,000 is oak and 20,000 is redwood.

Mrs. Waterman, Calistoga.—Total acres, 20; all in bearing; soil loam; vineyard low lying; crop, 30 tons.

S. C. Way, Calistoga.—Total, 15 acres; all in bearing; soil gravelly loam; vineyard low lying; crop, 20 tons.

W. York, Calistoga.—Total. 20 acres; all in bearing; soil loam; vineyard low lying; crop, 32 tons; cooperage, 50,000 gallons, of which 5,000 is oak and 45,000 is redwood.

A. Zoeller, Calistoga.—Total, 20 acres; all in bearing; soil loam; vineyard upland; crop, 35 tons; cooperage, 40,000 gallons, all of which is redwood.

Zoeller Estate, Calistoga.—Total, 20 acres; all in bearing; soil loam; vineyard low lying; crop. 30 tons.